SECRETS BEHIND THE PULPIT

SWEET TEE

MZ. LADY P PRESENTS, LLC

ACKNOWLEDGMENTS

I'm thankful to be able to continue this journey as an author. The feelings of being overwhelmed to perform at your best in all aspects of life have been tough. Sometimes one can only take a step back and recuperate in order to move forward. One doesn't realize how much work goes into producing a book and that all authors face different challenges. I've been learning more and more that consistency is the key. Grateful for all of the opportunities to come my way I continue to pray for the many more blessings to fall in my lap.

Thank you to all of the supporters and readers that have read my work. Special thanks to my mentors who I will not name for the continuous support and encouragement. I'm still learning about the author world as I make a name for myself. I spend hours researching, reading, and writing to perfect my craft. I would like to thank the other authors who work hard and produce dope books that inspire me to do better. All authors should be acknowledged because this job is tough. We cry, want to quit, and sometimes second guess. I have learned that a book cannot be rushed; it must be done right from beginning to end.

I am a proud member of Mz. Lady P Presents Publishing Co. under Patrice Williams, better known as National Best Selling Author,

Mz. Lady P. Shout out to my pen sisters and brother. Our family is growing and glowing with talent across the board. I'm proud of you all. I must give a shout out to Mz. Lady P for being a dope publisher and author. Thank you for always keeping it real and providing advice and motivation. You are a beast in this industry so to be a part of your team is a wonderful feeling. Thank you for seeing the potential in me during a difficult time in my life.

This continuous journey as a new author has been exciting, frustrating, and tiring but it is worth it! My dream has just begun and there is so much work to do. This is the fifth book I have completed. I want to thank my mother as she watches from heaven and continues to give me inspiration. There is not one day that goes by that I do not think about you. It is you who inspire some of my crazy characters from the stories you used to share about back in the day. Continue to watch over me and your son.

To those who have a dream, follow it and never give up! Push through and if you want it bad enough your hard work will pay off. The stories I write always have some type of message to it and it is my sincere hope that it inspires the readers. Living the life, we were dealt is easier said than done for some folks. Therefore, it's nice to get lost in others' drama via a good book. Each character created is based on friends, old associates, and from people watching.

Lastly, I would like to acknowledge myself for fighting against depression which is a struggle in my life. November and December are the worst months for me because it is a constant reminder of my mother's death. A hard pill to swallow almost three years later the struggle remains. Depression can consume you and turn you into a different person unless you fight it! I write to cope, I write to inspire, and I write to promote my story. All things are possible through Jesus Christ our Lord!

Love yours truly,
Sweet Tee

NOTE FROM THE AUTHOR

My inspiration for this book came from a combination of watching Greenleaf, personal experiences and reading the work of some great authors. It stirred up something in me to step out of my box with something different. I struggled with the idea to write this book because of the possible whispers or criticisms. After talking to my publisher and pen sisters, I decided to go ahead and do it.

In this day in age religion and churches have become so overrated among all ethnic groups. Specifically, in the black church where fashion and titles are more important than praising the Lord. Now before you bite my head off, think about a few things as I make my points clear. Think about the last time you went to church and the outfit you wore. Did you get or give someone a compliment based on the attire? Did you look at someone's outfit and instantly talk about them? What about how many times the collection plates come around?

I remember overhearing two women on Sunday morning talking about a woman who was no more than twenty years old. She had on a red dress that she had to tug at every time she stood up. It was obvious that she had a night out at the club but regardless, the two women were wrong. Even worse, I thought the same thing so I was just as guilty. People love to believe that church folks are incapable of committing sin.

This book is a reminder that we are all human beings. Even the leader of a congregation and his family are not excluded from sin nor is life as it seems to those looking in from the outside. Not every Christian household uses proper language or behaves in the manner church folks ought to, yet sit in the first pew every Sunday. Remember no one is perfect and we are all flawed.

KEEP UP WITH SWEET TEE

Facebook: Authoress Sweet Tee
   Readers Group: Sweet Tee's Reading Corner
   Instagram: sweettee3215
   Twitter: AuthoressSweetT
   Website: http://jonestt25.wixsite.com/sweettee

PROLOGUE

astor Charles Wallace

As a man of God, I lived like any other man, with sin and prayer to do better each day the Lord blessed me. Life as a pastor isn't as easy as people think it is; it's more than standing before the congregation quoting scripture. It was more than wearing the robe or collar and touting the Bible around. Passion was required to do the task and not every man or woman possessed it. Catering to everyone's needs was a 24/7 job that I was called to embrace yet found myself questioning why sometimes. The constant visits to hospitals, meetings on top of meetings, not to mention the deacon board meetings. The best legacy is a life spent in service to others and that is my sole duty.

Not always a saved man, I did a few things that were life lessons to not do again. After college I met my wife, Connie, and that is when it hit me to change my lifestyle. Although the initial marriage was a rough start; by the grace of God Connie and I worked things out. As a husband, I did everything possible by man to make her happy. Despite her past discretions with another man prior to our marriage, I forgave her without hesitation. Little did I know my own secret discretions would take me back down the path of destruction?

1

As a father, I did my best to give my time to the ladies in my life. With three daughters my job was to make sure they knew the church wasn't as important as they were to me. Tia, the eldest, moved out but occasionally visited for Sunday dinners. Lauren, the middle child, is smart and independent. Lastly, Gabrielle was the youngest who is a saint in my eye. She loved church just as much as me and it warmed my heart to watch her grow into a sweet young woman.

The Wallace family was far from perfect. I, as the leader, had to make sure our imperfections never reached the ears of those who attended Calvary Christian Life Baptist Church. A scandal was the last thing Calvary needed, especially under my leadership. One who preached the word couldn't then turn around and do the opposite. Yet sometimes it is easier said than done. Temptation was a powerful thing that grabbed a hold to any man even men of the cloth.

This book will introduce you to my family, our secrets and the journey we went through battling the devil and each other. Secrets behind the pulpit reveal that saints are sinners too, even me. No one is perfect and until we all grasp that concept, no one has the right to cast a stone at others for their choices and mistakes. Too often we point the finger at others instead of at ourselves. We are only human, so of course we fall short, but as a child of God, all things are possible through Christ our Lord. Forgiveness, change, and acceptance are the moral of this story.

* * *

A FORTY-MINUTE PHONE call held me longer than expected making me a few minutes late to the deacon board meeting. I grabbed my legal pad and pen quickly made my way to the boardroom. "Sorry I'm late, continue Deacon Brown."

"You all were given a copy of the proposal along with the budget. It is our responsibility to provide for our congregation. "Someone get a copy to the pastor," Deacon Brown ordered as he gazed at me. I took my seat directly across from him as Deacon Black sat to the right of me.

"We need to make a lot of improvements in this church starting with the pew cushions, new computers for the kids, and lastly new hymn books."

"I agree, we can place orders for those items, not a big problem. It's the building fund and proposal I'm concerned about," I said cutting my eye at Deacon Black who sat with his arms folded. I scanned the room as I continued to speak my mind. "How do several flat-screen televisions be a part of the building fund? When did praising the Lord become so materialistic?" I asked in a rhetorical tone.

He cleared his throat before he spoke "Umm there is enough money to get two things fixed at a time. Our church needs a fix that is all we trying to do here. With these young folks, we need ways to keep them around the building. The money would be used strictly for the church."

"I truly believe that however let's not forget the reputation Deacon Edwards left us with. Our budget must remain intact therefore, I'm in agreement with the pastor," Deacon Brown said then sat back in the black leather chair with his hands folded. Suddenly, the two got into a disagreement about the way communion is done. I had a headache with their bickering back and forth about the building proposal. I swear it was like working with a bunch of big babies the way they carried on. As a leader of the congregation, the role as pastor was more than preaching a sermon on Sundays. The job required patience, lack of sleep, and working with people from all walks of life.

"NO, NO, NO, NO, Deacon Black. Absolutely not! We can't afford another mishap like two years ago. The amount of debt this church was in was beyond embarrassing. For that, you and the deacon board will have to come up with another proposal.

"C'mon Pastor," Deacon Black shouted as his hands hit the table. Everyone in the room looked around to see what would happen next. Deacon Black continued, "Need I remind you of 1 Timothy 3:8-12? We the board handle money affairs so we should be able to spend how we see fit."

With the palm of my hands, I pushed myself back in the chair on wheels. I stood up to address the group. "Yes, you were all chosen to be in the position on this deacon board but please remember who truly runs this church. Not me, you, or anyone else, this is God's house. With that being said, if there aren't any other pressing matters, I need to go back to my office. Quiet filled the room instead head nods up and down sufficed as an answer. "Angela can you please join me, there is something I need your help with." I collected my pad, pen, and the proposal and made my way out of the boardroom. Back to my office Angela sat at her station and typed the minutes on her Rose Gold MacBook. I requested this to ensure a record of agenda items. I entered my office and closed the door behind me.

My spirit told me to give Tia a quick call. She was on my mind, nor had I heard from her. I picked up the receiver and dialed her number from the landline, praying she answered. The second she answered her voice didn't sound like the chipper happy to talk usual tone. Although our conversation began dry and dull, by the end of the call she loosened up and I imagined her smiling through the phone. When she said those three words "Love ya daddy," all of the troubles of the day disappeared. Tia had a good heart and was just misunderstood sometimes.

* * *

LEANED BACK in the chocolate brown leather chair a knock at the door prompted me to sit up straight. "Come in," I yelled as Angela walked in leaving the door opened. She always tried to wear clothing that wasn't too provocative or misleading, but nothing worked. No matter what she wore she couldn't hide her figure or bosoms. Lord knows I tried to keep my eyes on my computer screen but it wasn't easy. We were distracted by the deacons' voices that echoed "Good night pastor," in passing through the hallway.

"Pastor, did you need anything before I shut down my computer? The minutes are printing right now."

"No. We are done for the night."

The sound of the printer ran in the background as I watched her hover over her computer. Then she retrieved the papers from the machine. Left, right, left, her hips sashayed back and forth giving me the vision of booty. Quickly I swallowed and diverted my eyes down by the time she turned around to face me. "Pastor here is a copy of the notes from tonight's meeting. Let me just say Deacon Black really has it out for you, what is that all about?" Expecting an answer, she looked at me.

"Umm, all I can say is sometimes those closest to you pray for your downfall. Not to speak badly about him, but he feels like he should be the pastor instead of me. I never understood his obsession. My job is no cake walk, it's long hours and constant service."

"He doesn't have that tone of voice or deliverance you do. Besides, it takes a certain kind of man to lead; that man is you, pastor." I tried not to blush at her comment because it made me feel good inside. I straightened up my desk, we grabbed our bags and she turned the light off and closed the door behind her. With the alarm set, we made our way out the building and over to her black Ford Focus. The only thing I could think of was sex. I recited different scriptures and bible quotes silently to help fight the urge, but it only helped so much. With a quick check on the time, Connie expected me home soon.

"Pastor, I have a project at my house that requires a man's touch. It's too late to ask for your help, but it really needs to get done. Can you help me?"

I wasn't sure Angela really had a project, but I agreed regardless. "All right, I will follow behind you to your house."

"Great. I won't keep you too long, but this can't wait much longer. It has been long overdue."

Once inside my vehicle, I gave myself a pep talk to not let the devil use me. My intentions were to perform an act of kindness. When I pulled up behind her on the street, I noticed a quiet neighborhood as I looked around, getting out. With the key in hand, she unlocked and entered.

"Please take your shoes off upon entering, thank you."

"Should I take off anything else while I'm at it?"

"Just your shoes for now."

I closed her door and locked it as she gave me a quick tour of her well-organized home. Her home was big enough for five people, yet she lived alone and I wondered why.

"Why do you live in this big house alone?"

"Sometimes people fall down on their luck and need a place to rest their head. I provide that to those who need help here and there."

"Oh, that's pretty dope! You are a sweet person for doing that!"

"Well are we going to talk or you ready to get your hands dirty?"

"I guess I'm ready to work."

"Well follow me upstairs," she insisted as I gladly obliged. When she pushed the door opened, the large queen bed with four bed posts and matching footlocker at the foot caught my full attention.

"Welcome to the place where I unwind after a long day of dealing with folks."

Right there on the spot she unzipped her dress and let it drop to the floor as I watched. My eyes blinked double time as she exposed her figure to me without hesitancy.

"Don't just stand their honey, I need your help unhooking my bra."

"Wow," is all I could say as my manhood got rock hard through my khaki pants as she stood in her blue teal lace Victoria Secret bra and panty set.

"You probably wanted to see what was under the long dresses; now you have your glimpse."

With enough staring, I leaned in to kiss her neck, earlobes, and those soft fun bags that sat atop of her. I unhooked her bra then slide her panties down. My hands caressed her arms, back, and ass. When she grabbed my piece, I fell in love with that woman, swear.

"Ahh yeah, that feels nice Angie," I moaned ready to get inside of her.

"Well take off those clothes and let me see what you have to offer big boy!"

I began by coming out of my shirt and pants followed by the t-shirt, but she insisted on taking my boxers off. By her body language and facial expressions, I assumed she liked what she saw too. With my snake exposed, Angie's warm hand gripped it as if she owned it. I was beyond horny, ready to sex her for as long as I could last.

"This is your one and only chance to have fun with me in efforts to stop your wandering eyes. I will make a small confession to you that must never be repeated to anyone else. You are special, and I saw something in you that I didn't see in others. To be honest, I've had impure thoughts about you, and usually, I would never do something like this."

"I feel the same way about you, and I've felt so bad and guilty. It's unbelievable that we shared that in common. My wife just hasn't pleased me in the way I desired. Now to see you naked, to touch you, kiss you, is like finding water after three days. I want you so bad Angie."

I rubbed between her thighs in a soft and intimate manner to loosen and relax her legs. They parted effortlessly. It took me a second to find the spot until I put her arms up as she laid on her back. I found my stroke then pounded her until we couldn't sin anymore. In the bed of a stranger, I expected to feel guilty, instead it was the opposite. Doing wrong felt so right, that I needed to do it one more time with Angela, who was at least seven years younger than my wife. The swivel of her hips while on top of my rod took me on a mind-blowing journey. I was officially hooked on this woman.

Angela put me to sleep with her hypnotizing sex. It was too late to go home by the time I focused to notice the time and missed calls. Out of twenty something years of marriage, this was the first time I stayed out all night without as much as a call or text.

"Damn it, my wife is going to kill me for staying out all night," I said out loud as Angela woke up.

"Just tell her you worked so hard that you fell asleep in your office on the couch. Your job is stressful and tiresome, but you deserve to have alone time away from her."

"Hmm, you sound like you've done this before. You think she will accept that lie?"

"I assume she would since you haven't given her a reason to lie before. It's highly unlikely that she showed up at the church looking for you. If so, you have a problem," she joked.

Angela provided me with a washcloth and soap to clean myself up with some non-deodorized soap. She claimed it would help keep Connie's suspicions to a minimum. It was apparent she was no stranger to pulling tricks like this, and it made me feel a little dirty and used. As a member of the church, no one could find out about this secret. My image had to be protected; there couldn't be any type of scandal tied to my name or family.

All of a sudden, the guilt made me wonder why I made the mistake of entering another woman other than my wife. I tried to act normal but had to rush out of there the moment a peep of sunlight rose.

"CHARLES WALLACE, where in the world were you last night? I was worried sick about you! You didn't reply to my texts or calls," Connie shouted when I walked through the entrance door.

"Baby I'm so sorry about that. I fell asleep on the couch in my office. After the deacon board meeting, I was worn out by Deacon Black, not to mention prep for the Atlanta trip. My eyes were so heavy I thought it best to just sleep in the church rather get on the road. It was a judgment call, but I should have called you. I'm sorry."

"I'm just glad you are safe. God must have been tired of me talking his ears off. Go get cleaned up while I fix you breakfast."

"Perfect. It will be time for me to leave again for a few hours."

With a deep sigh, Connie mumbled, "The life we live, huh, sometimes I want you to myself."

"We will do a date night very soon I promise. I love you, First Lady Wallace."

"I love you back. Now go get ready."

The smile vanished once up the stairs out her eyesight. Disgusted with my adultery, it was my first time sleeping with another woman. Angela and I shouldn't have crossed that line. I wasn't the guy who slept around because my love for Connie was too deep. Being pastor didn't keep me and my wife from having sex, but my addiction made me crave more than I could ask of her. The steaming hot water and

Axe body wash cleansed Angela off of me. Nonetheless, the thoughts weren't as easy to erase.

Though I was clean, I still felt dirty from sin as I stood in the mirror and dried off with the royal blue bath towel. I applied deodorant under each arm, slapped lotion over my body then slipped on my boxers. From the bathroom, I entered the walk-in closet to choose a suit to wear. Settling on a tan suit, I dressed and headed back downstairs. Connie stood across from me as she leaned over the island countertop and watched me eat the food she prepared. At one point I was a bit paranoid that she knew what I did. Women had a special way of sniffing out a lie.

To break the silence, I engaged in small talk. "Baby I was thinking we should do something special, like a mini trip away. Think about it while I'm at the church."

"I'll think about it. I gotta go meet Juanita. Love you," she answered. With a quick peck on the lips, she walked away. The very touch of her lips on mine made the guilt worse.

In the same position for over half an hour, the sound of my cell made me remove myself from the kitchen seat. Distracted by my recent actions, I hadn't noticed the time pass by making me late to the hospital. Quickly, I gathered my items and jetted out the connecting door to the garage. It was my turn to serve communion and fellowship with Ms. Irene, a longtime member, whose health had begun to deteriorate. Sweet and alert; she always managed to keep her spirits up despite the battles she faced. By the time I parked and took the elevator to her room, she was sitting in the cushioned rocking chair crocheting.

"Sorry I'm late Ms. Irene, I lost track of time. How are you feeling today?"

"Blessed and highly favored son! Come on in and have a seat."

"Amen to that ma'am!" I sat with the communion wafers and grape juice as we recited the Lord's Supper prayer together. For an entire hour, she held my undivided attention as we talked about the ways of the world. By the time I left, my spirits were in a much clear space and the guilt I once concealed had vanished. That was until I arrived home to find Connie went out of her way to surprise me. Marvin Gaye played in the background as she sat in my favorite chair wearing next to nothing. Mini Twix candy bars formed a heart on the bed with rose petals scattered throughout the room. I got undressed to fulfill my husbandly duties, while Angela remained in the back of my head.

onnie Wallace
	Image was everything to me especially being the pastor's wife, but it wasn't easy. There were many days I wanted to lose my religion or bit my tongue. Before I reacted, I had to realize as a woman of God, it was my duty to be the bigger person and smile. Juanita talked me into yoga and of course, there was no backing out of it. She claimed it would help with my issues. I decided to take a yoga class several times a month. It has done wonders for me. Not to mention, it gets me away from home and the church. Don't get me wrong, I love my life and lifestyle, however, a woman needs time alone. Motherhood was great since I didn't have any little ones to look after.

* * *

EVERY MORNING, I sat at my desk facing the window with a cup of strong, black coffee and my Bible for daily devotion. My office had the best view of a medium size Crimson King Maple colored tree. It was something about the peace and quiet that helped me receive my task of the day. My role as a mother, wife, and first lady kept me busy.

As a forty-seven-year-old African American woman, success and image were important to me. Regardless of being a woman of God, I cared about what people thought and said about me. Materialistic, my love for being the best dressed with a nice huge home made me feel better. The life I lived seemed like a dream to some but to me, it was a blessing and curse.

My husband's life was mine; everything he dealt with included me. We were one and I supported him as the leader of Calvary. As a spiritual leader, he needed support and encouragement. I too, carried the weight of the church. I read over his sermons, let him vent, and even brainstormed together. Charles and I were one in the same: anything he did reflected on me and vice versa. It's a good thing my deepest dark secret is safe from the knowledge of our congregation. Lost in another world, I raised my coffee cup to my lips only to notice it was empty. At the same time, Pastor entered the room. His soft lips pressed against my cheek as he delivered a five-second kiss.

"Morning baby! I knew I would find you in here. What are you working on?"

"It's time to plan the fundraiser event to raise awareness about Lupus. Sandra will come over to help with planning."

"Well, you ladies will have a quiet place to work, I'm going to the hospital for a few hours to serve communion and worship."

"What do you have a taste for, so dinner can be ready?"

"Umm, if it's no troublesome stuffed jumbo shells with meat and cheese. Bless you and your hands woman. Something messy yet tasty will do me justice later."

"See you whenever you make it back. Check the microwave if you get in after nine tonight. Love you."

With Charles out the house, I went upstairs to the bedroom in search for a few pictures from the Annual Lupus Fundraiser last year. The first box in eyesight was at the back of my closet. Clutching the box from the shelf, the lid fell off. Pictures from my college days sat right on top forcing me to chuckle. Ready to go down memory lane my butt connected with my steel grey chaise lounge. Shuffling through the old school photographs, two in particular, took me back to my junior year at Spelman College: a historically Black college. I was a third generation, young, full of life and dreams, the world was in the palm of my hands.

It was 1992 at the Spelman/Morehouse Homecoming event when Charles and I had our first encounter. Huh, he was not attractive at all. He had just graduated from Morehouse College, popular with a semi cocky attitude. Morehouse men tended to be smooth brothas who were the dressed to impress, all about the business, type. After several attempts during the parade and game, he finally gave up trying to talk to me. It was the last time we saw each other until a month later. My travel from Atlanta to Milwaukee, Wisconsin for Thanksgiving, turned out to be a dreadful surprise.

Apparently, Charles parents were old friends of my parents-- all alumni of Spelman and Morehouse. Imagine my face when they attended Thanksgiving dinner with our family. My mother used that opportunity to push me onto to Charles as if she had a prearranged agreement or something. Her persistence for me to sit next to him annoyed the heck out of me, but it didn't stop there. His parents were high-class, uppity folks that were even more of a turn-off. During dinner was the first time in a long time I kept my mouth closed for more than twenty minutes. In return, my facial expressions spoke for me, as it was clear I had no plans to cooperate. To make a long story short, from that day forward both, families pushed and pushed until a union between Charles and me happened.

The more time went by, we learned to gradually get to know each other. Shortly afterward I found out I was pregnant with Tia. Everyone was excited, yet the truth behind my pregnancy involved another man. Joseph Moore-- my high school sweetheart, was the father of my child. We had been intimate before the marriage to Charles, so there was no doubt Joseph was the father. He didn't take the union too well and insisted we continued to see each other. To this day Joseph isn't aware that Tia is his biological daughter and honestly--I'm glad. Could you imagine the scandal that would arise within the church?

Before I knew it, an hour had passed so I put the box away and continued my search for the fundraiser items. Another fifteen minutes later with no luck, I called it a quits. With Charles out doing hospital visits to a few elderlies of Calvary, I decided to invite Sandra over to work on the Fourth Annual Lupus Fundraiser. She was a part of the planning committee. Though the event was still far away, it was never too early to plan. This was a special event because it helped raise money and awareness for those who suffer from Lupus.

When the bell rang, I hustled from the kitchen to open the door. "Come right in Sandra, make yourself comfortable. Would you like some tea?" we gave each other a half hug.

"Thanks. I have a binder from last year with documentation of everything from the planning to the invoices for catering. Yes, tea sounds wonderful. Connie, I can't get over how lovely your home always looks. It's like something from a Home Living Magazine. Did you have a decorator come out? Oh, I'm sorry, where are my manners?"

Instantly she stopped talking and just smiled. "Oh, stop it, Sandra, it flatters me how much you admire the place. Cleaning these rooms is the downside to owning a home this size. I'm sure your home is as lovely. Let's work from the patio area where the ideas can flow," I insisted.

"Works for me. Can I help with anything?"

"No thank you. Come with me to the kitchen area, I'll prep a lite snack for us while we work."

"Okay. May I have honey for my tea? Thanks.

"Sure. Take a seat and get comfortable."

The smile never left my face as Sandra's words made me feel pride in my home. I filled the tea kettle with water and sat it on the stove to boil. The five-bedroom place took a lot of upkeep; not to mention cleaning which I did myself instead of having a maid. I placed a wooden tray on the Calcutta marble counter, followed by two cups each with a Lipton green tea bags and a small bottle of honey.

"So, what's new with your family? Your granddaughter was such a cute acolyte on Sunday. Bless her heart."

"Amelia is an angel but her mother, huh Connie. That daughter of mine is struggling to stay clean. It puzzles me on where I went wrong. I gave her love, discipline, and prayed for her daily. Just don't understand it," Sandra said as she gazed down in embarrassment.

"No, don't go blaming yourself, these kids know right from wrong. As a parent you did your duty, it is the child's responsibility to act with common sense. The older they become, the more trouble sometimes." The kettle started to whistle taking my attention away from Sandra momentarily. Retrieving the kettle, I filled our cups and sat the pot back on the stove. We continued to chat over the sound of my clinking spoon as I stirred the thick gold honey.

"I think this year we should make gift bags stuffed with heart shaped bracelets, t-shirts, and other giveaways items."

"Yes, this year the shirts should be purple long sleeve with white letters. Last year they were white with purple letters. I think alternating between the two has worked out." Sandra flipped through the binder to the page of the shirt proof from last year.

"Renee said she will be able to attend the event and serve as the keynote speaker this year. Remember her brother dealt with Lupus up until the day the Lord called him home."

"Great to hear! Having her there will really help the cause and spread more awareness." I sipped my tea as the warm liquid slid down my throat smoothly.

"If you don't have any objections, I think we should use the same vendor from last year."

"None at all. They accommodated our group even with last minute issues and earned their check. I'm curious on catering though, we cannot have them running out of chicken at an all-black event." Sandra and I laughed so hard at my comment.

"Well you can check on some alternative catering companies who will not charge an arm and leg. If we book within the next few months, we might get a discount or something."

"Sounds like a plan. I'll do some searching around for the top three recommended services. Otherwise, we'll have to double check on the chicken orders to ensure enough is served."

"I agree. Just let me know if you need assistance. Is that clock correct?"

"Yes, it is."

"Oh! I need to go pick Amelia up from her other grandmother's house. She has been there for two days visiting her father's side of the family. Bless their hearts, they have been supportive in all of this."

"I'm glad Amelia has grandparents like you two who give her love and support. It was nice getting together. I'll do some work on my end and touch base in a few weeks." I accompanied her back down the hallway to the door.

"Thank you, Connie, for listening to my troubles. As a mother, I knew you wouldn't mind. I'll talk to you soon. Have a blessed day."

"Same to you, Sandra. Remember I'm just a phone call away if you need to vent, cry, or whatever. Give that grandbaby a hug for me." With the door cracked, I watched her get inside the car and pull off. I stood for a few minutes to absorb the sun and overall beautiful September day. I went back inside and did some odds and ends around the house then took a long lunch break.

CHAPTER 2

astor Charles Wallace
        I learned something shocking about my daughter, Tia, who in return learned something about me. Daughters held their dads on a pedestal, and for her to see me in an environment known as the devil's playground-- was the worst. Even though I hadn't done anything but set foot in the place, I was guilty by association because of the deacons.

I sat in my office on a Saturday night prepping for service tomorrow morning. With my bible in front of me, my yellow legal pad remained blank. The sermon couldn't be forced, it had to come from my spirit, and it had to move the congregation. Flashbacks from Friday night of my daughter on stage clouded my mind. It was hard to keep that image out of my head, she was my little girl dressed half-naked, parading for strange men. It was so stupid of me to go with Deacon Black and Deacon Brown to a gentlemen's club. What was supposed to have been an innocent night out turned into a regretful mistake! Neither of them disclosed the fact that we were going to such a place until we arrived.

Rather than sit in the car I, entered the Landing Strip Lounge. Right away, the variety of women dancing and swinging from poles put me in a trance while I recited James 1:13-18. Temptation caught me for a short time; I gawked as I liked what was before my eyes letting sin win the battle. From the deacons' behavior, it was clear they were regulars, even more of a reason to stay away from them if it wasn't work-related. Learning something new about the two men proved they couldn't be trusted with handling church money. To avoid causing a scene, I followed behind them to a table and took a seat. It was then; I saw my daughter shaking what her mama gave her. The good thing was that neither Deacon Black or Brown knew it was Tia.

Before I proceed with the story, I want to take you back to when Angela and I shared a platonic relationship. Before the impure thoughts invaded me like they did at the Landing Strip, she was purely my assistant and nothing more. Angela knocked on the door that caused me to lift my head up. She stood in the doorframe wearing a long, navy blue dress that did no justice hiding her shape. Her body was beyond stacked up top and in the back. I did my best to keep my mind from going to the gutter.

"Hi, Angela. What can I do for you dear?"

"I'm on my way out, Pastor. I just wanted to let you know the church is emptied. Please don't stay much longer and get home safe."

"Before you leave may I ask you something?"

"Sure."

"My vision for the sermon tomorrow isn't coming easily to me tonight. Do you have any suggestions, anything you feel deeply about?"

"Well, this week has been challenging, trying not to lose my cool because of dumb people and their actions. Pastor, I hold my tongue and recite a prayer in my head to keep from losing my religion," she giggled.

"Understood. There are people in this world who are unhappy, so they try to inflict that unhappiness on others. You know the saying, "misery loves company." You are not responsible for the way others behave. Resist stooping low and instead, show kindness or remove yourself from the situation."

"Pastor, you have always been a nice, caring, and compassionate man-- who I've grown to like. You are a good father, husband, and God fearing. I just wish more men were like you."

"Angela, I'm not perfect...not by a long shot," I uttered softly as my thoughts went back to Tia. Her secret life left me stunned and hurt me at the same time and vice versa.

"Pastor, I have to get going now but I hope my words were able to help you with the sermon idea. Many people believe in you, follow you, and most importantly: they believe the word you preach. Don't let the people down."

"You have given me the inspiration needed to write the sermon for service."

"I'm glad to help. Have a good night, Pastor."

"You too, Angela," I said as she exited the office. Angela reminded me of something I witnessed during a hospital visit. The spirit guided my heart and hands until the message I drafted titled *"Don't Let Em Steal Your Joy"* was complete. Satisfied,

It was a little after nine o'clock and I was glad to be home with my loved ones. The moment I walked through the door and walked over the threshold, the troubles of my day vanished. I walked up the stairs on the left side of the double staircase that lead to the part of the house reserved for my wife and me. Pushing the door open Connie sat in her hand cushioned wooden rocking chair with a book. Dressed in her pink lace nightgown, she had her hair in a bun with her glasses on. She looked like a naughty schoolteacher when she wore those glasses. All of the impure thoughts I had about Angela were out of my head once my wife looked at me. I bent over to kiss her.

"Good evening, Honey, I was wondering what time you would get in."

"I had trouble coming up with the perfect sermon for tomorrow's message. Not to mention Deacon Black constantly harassing me."

"Aww poor Pastor, you knew Deacon Black was a handful when you decided to keep him around. Nevertheless, pray on it, and it will work out."

I undressed down to my boxers. When I turned to look at her she was so into her book, it made me curious.

"What are you reading? You are so into that book like you can't read it tomorrow."

"This book is too good to put down right now! It's an urban fiction book by a collection of authors under Mz. Lady P Presents. It's called *Love in Different Area Codes: A Valentine's Day Affair.*"

"I don't even want to know what that book is about--I'm sure of that. While you are reading that sinful stuff, I hope you ready for church in the morning," I said on the way to the bathroom for a quick shower. Connie was a night owl like myself. So, some nights we would talk, read, or share our inner thoughts. She moved to the bed by the time I came from the bathroom. The moment my body slid in the bed, the night heated up. Connie must have felt more than the spirit; perhaps she had inspiration from her book. Either way, I was a happy man.

My wife was on her best behavior during the day, but at night--oh the freak comes out of her. Our fun time at night is another reason why our home is split off from the children. Connie and I were at an age where sex was a part of our activity together as a couple. After all, we were married with three children. Connie put that sweet loving on me so good, I went to sleep instantly.

The next morning, I was up by five-forty for a quick workout in the basement to get my blood pumping. It was mandatory for me to exercise every morning to minimize the physical and exhaustion caused by being a pastor. My routine included: the treadmill for fifteen minutes, weights for ten minutes, and then a cool down. By the time I made it back upstairs, my wife had just gotten out of the shower as I was about to hop in.

Sunday morning came before I knew it. Nevertheless, I praised God for another day. I rolled over to face my Nubian queen, who was awake blinking as she stared at me.

"Good morning baby! You are such a beautiful creation God made just for me."

"You are too kind, Pastor," Connie smirked as she gave me a kiss on the cheek.

"I'll start breakfast and wake the girls up while you get clean."

"Thank you, baby," my voice projected from the shower. It didn't take me long to soap up, clean myself from the sweat, and funk to be refreshed and ready to preach the word of God. With the towel wrapped around my waist, I proceeded to shave my face while rehearsing my sermon. Groomed and dressed in a black solid classic fit Ralph Lauren suit, I headed for the kitchen. Lauren bumped into me as we scrambled down the stairs before Connie yelled. "Morning baby girl."

"Morning daddy," she replied followed with a hug. Lauren reminded me of Tia sometimes, which made me wonder if she had secrets too. All young ladies hide things from their parents; therefore, I couldn't handle any more craziness from my girls. We accompanied each other only to find my youngest already at the table

"Hi sweetheart," I addressed her followed by a peck on the fore-head. Gabby was so innocent, at least that's what I hoped for anyway. As a father, having a son was something every man wanted, however, the Lord sent me three girls instead.

"Honey, do you want orange juice or coffee?" Connie inquired in the midst of sitting my plate on the table.

"Orange juice, please." The four of us sat at the table as Gabby blessed the food.

"Dear heavenly Father. We thank you for this day. Thank you for the meal we are about to receive to nourish our body. In your name, we pray, amen."

"Amen."

Refreshed with a clear mind, I prayed for forgiveness not just for me but for Tia. As a father, I loved all of the daughters and tried to be that perfect parent; the man who taught them right from wrong. Ever since Friday night, the idea of my baby girl dancing for money, was an issue that had to be resolved. I pushed the thought to the back of my head to enjoy the meal with my family. Connie sat across from me, sipping her coffee with her pinky extended. Without a word, my eyes moved from my plate to my wife until she broke the silence.

"Baby why do you keep staring at me? Is there egg on my face or something," she asked rubbing her mouth.

"No. You are just that stunning to me! He who finds a wife finds a good thing," I spoke and blew her an air kiss. She was definitely a good thing for me. It's hard to believe that we once were forced to marry and love each other by our parents. Over the years, Connie has been my backbone, best friend, and lover. If only she knew what I did behind her back when I'm supposed to be out visiting the sick or hosting bible study.

"Amen. You know how to flatter me, honey. I guess I got lucky too, ha," she teased.

"Please don't start that mushy mess," Lauren expressed with a piece of bacon in her hand.

"Oh child, stop it. How you think you were conceived? Besides, ain't nothing wrong with a married couple partaking in a little flirting," Connie blurted in a joking tone.

"Ugh. I'll be outside until it's time to leave," Lauren uttered as she and Gabby carried their empty dishes to the dishwasher.

"Your father and I will be out momentarily." As my wife slide her chair back from the table to collect her plate, I interjected to clear the table for her. I loaded the dishwasher, careful not to get dirty, then went to use the downstairs bathroom one last time. Just as I picked up my bible and car keys from the mantel, the phone rang. E. Black scrolled across the screen, which prompted me to answer.

"Deacon Black on my way out the door, what can I do for you this morning?"

"First off, good morning, Pastor. I pray all is well with your family. I'm calling to inform you of something that might turn into trouble."

"Let me stop you there, Deacon, this will have to wait until after service today. I appreciate your call, but my mind must remain clear. Whatever it is; I'm sure you can handle it on my behalf. We can talk later."

"It's regarding Deacon Brown, but I will put it on the back burner.

Trust me, you will need to hear me out on this matter. It could affect the entire church."

"Oh? We can meet in detail on Tuesday before the deacon board meeting. Now I really have to go, see you in church."

"Alright, Pastor," he said in a nonchalant tone before the call was disconnected.

With a shake of the head I proceeded to walk out the door. The girls waited by my navy blue Yukon truck. The three of us climbed inside as the sound of the doors closing followed. With Connie still inside the house, I took the time to openly talk to Lauren and Gabby. As a father, it was important for them to know I loved them and would always make time for them.

"So, girls talk to me. What's new? Let's chat before your mom comes out."

"Umm, working at Best Buy isn't too bad anymore, but people are crazy. This one guy had a meltdown because we didn't have a specific type of game controller."

"Wow over a game controller? Your generation is a bit dramatic, Dear. Gabby, honey, you're quiet."

"Nothing new with me daddy," Gabby said quickly as she sat in the back seat directly behind me. Connie finally sashayed in the direction of the truck which was perfect timing, because we had to be the first to arrive to set up before nine o'clock.

CHAPTER 3

*T*ia Wallace

As a kid, you could say I was an ugly duckling with big glasses, pigtails, with blotchy skin from eczema. By the time I reached puberty, lost the glasses, and began to develop--boys wouldn't leave me alone. The older I got, the cuter I became and my confidence made me feel like the most beautiful girl in the world.

Fast forward, I'm twenty-three years old and I'm a professor during the day and an exotic dancer at night. If my mom found out, she would fall to the floor from embarrassment and shock. Unashamed of my night profession, dancing gave me an adrenaline rush that aided my addiction and need for attention.

Growing up as the pastor's kid there were eyes on me all the time, but it didn't matter to me because I did what I wanted to. Yes, a stoner, sinner, and the daughter of a pastor; I was still a good person. It always made me mad to hear people talk bad about exotic dancers and strippers, or those who just didn't respect the hustle. It was a job like any other job, but I made money each night. My only concern was running into someone who knew my family. Nevertheless, it pleasured me to feel unrestricted and free like a butterfly.

Some of you might be wondering if I suffered from some type of abuse resulting in my actions. The answer is no. You may also wonder how long it would be before men grew tired of me or vice versa. Becoming an exotic dancer was supposed to be something that occupied my time at night, but it turned into a two-year gig. The money got good; which prompted me to keep dancing. As the saying goes, "Money is the root of all evil," and a chick like me loved Washington, Jackson, Grant, and most importantly, Mr. Franklin. Each time I performed or swung on the pole, the money was validation that men liked the services I provided.

The Landing Strip Lounge wasn't bad because the men were respectable and didn't try that funny mess. Mostly regulars occupied the establishment and had their favorite dancers. Security was tight and did their job to the letter which made the dancers feel safe. Two men stood at the entrance doors at all times. Multiple men walked the floors to monitor the VIP sections and made sure things ran smoothly. Overall, the establishment was decent and was operated by a woman, Chastity-- how ironic right?

It was Friday: in the summer that meant the night could go either way. Dressed in loose leg jeans, a graphic t-shirt, and a long sleeve hoodie, I walked quickly inside straight into the changing room. By the time my eyelashes and makeup were done, the other girls began to flock in with their gossip and chatter on who and what they did last night. In my claimed territory closest to the door, my eyes scanned each girl as she passed by.

"What up Coco, girl you ready to get paid," Nadia shouted with her ratchet tail as I saw ass cheeks reflected through the mirror.

"I'm always ready to take a man's money, honey! Tonight should be interesting though, both of my cash cows might be here."

"Aye, clean them pockets girl."

We both busted out in laughter in the process of checking my face one last time. Dressed in my black and silver Go-Go top and bottoms, I did one more look in the mirror and dropped it low to get my legs ready. Upon walking out of the room, I stopped to make sure the DJ had my music then made my way to the bar for three shots of Vodka. It was time to warm up with a few private dances before hitting the stage. Within five minutes of walking the floor, Lance appeared and threw his hand in the air to catch my attention. In his late thirties, he stayed loaded with dough and loved Black women. Not too many blue-eyed white men caught my attention or made me wet. It was something different about his stride, the thin goatee he kept trimmed neatly, and the way he licked his lips.

"Damn, Coco, why are you so freaking gorgeous? Every time I step foot in this place you are the only person I want to see."

Inches away from each other's face, the tantalizing smell of his cologne filled my nostrils. *Damn, he smells so freaking good,* I thought as I smiled. "I'm glad to hear that boo! Let's move over to our usual spot for a private dance or two"

"Lead the way, pretty lady."

My hand connected with his as he followed me to the left side of the room not too far from the stage. He sat down on the cushioned seat, assumed the position, and enjoyed the sway of my hips. The more my ass cheeks jumped back and forth, the more he stuffed my shorts with fifty-dollar bills until he ran out.

"Coco, if you were my lady; anything you ever wanted, would be yours. Not to step on your toes, but you deserve the world."

"Honey, you already do every time you visit and I thank you for it. In all honesty, you are the first white guy with a cool vibe I've come in contact with in a while. But you know we can't cross lines."

"Only time will tell but until then bend over one more time, so I can tip you properly now."

I complied as he shoved more money inside my top. "Sorry to end this dance but I need to get ready for this song. Like always, it was a pleasure-- but you know how the routine goes. I need to get ready to hit the stage."

"It must be my lucky night! I'm going to the restroom then I'm coming closer to watch you."

"Enjoy the show," I answered back. Quickly I made it to the back to lock up my tips and for a quick outfit swap into a red bodysuit. It crossed in the front with an open back. Wiping any extra moisture from my body it was show time as the DJ began to play my song and introduced me to the stage.

Loose off Grey Goose, I took the stage to perform my routine by Beyoncé's "Dance for You". I swayed my hips from left to right, swirled, twisted, and dipped it low. The men went crazy whistling as all eyes were on me. To get out of my shell, I just imagined myself dancing in a full-body mirror. Each performance turned out perfect enough to get that money.

In the midst of my routine, I noticed a few older men taking a seat towards the front. Those older men's faces looked so familiar, however; my concern was those singles, twenties, and other bills filling the stage. Taking to the pole for a few more tricks the continuous whistles hyped me up to finish off strong. I moved to the floor in a provocative and sexy, luring way. In the process of moving closer and closer to edge where Lance stood, those familiar faces became a nightmare to my eyes. The lighting provided me enough light to notice my own father. *Oh, hell no! That is my daddy with Deacon Black and Deacon Brown. Shit! Keep dancing,"* was all I thought.

My heart raced and my palms sweaty as shock took hold of me, but money was the name of the game. I quickly finished like a professional, gathered the dead presidents from the floor, and rushed off the stage. Count that as the worst night of my life because I was embarrassed, flabbergasted, not to mention-- let down. Seeing my father's face out there crushed my heart. Never in a million years would I have believed this if someone tried to tell me.

To avoid being seen I quickly dressed, grabbed my cash and managed to locate Chastity to pay my house fees before bolting out the back door. Unexpectedly, my father was outside leaned against my 2016 Fathom blue Tesla with his arms folded.

"TIA NICOLE WALLACE! What in the devil are you doing at a place like this? Your mother and I raised you better!" he yelled as he put fear in me with his husky voice. He had never called me by my full name unless he was furious or disappointed in me.

"Huh, you and the deacons are in the wrong too! So, don't lecture me without explaining your own actions." Closer to him, I stood there with my weight shifted on the left leg all while avoiding eye contact.

"Looks like we both learned something tonight-- we can't keep secrets forever," I stated then walked over and opened the driver's door. Before hopping inside, I looked straight at him with saddened eyes, "Dad I love you, but this is too much right now. Please give me some space." Overwhelmed with the situation, I had to bounce immediately and without thinking drove to my best friend's house. Queenetta was the only person who would listen and understand my position. Close to two in the morning, I drove right into her driveway all cloudy headed. I needed her advice and smoking alone was no fun given the situation at hand. In the process of exiting the vehicle, I stood at her doorstep like a lost puppy in need of shelter.

Knock! Knock! Knock!

Minutes later, Queen opened the door wearing some red plaid men boxers with a matching tank. She also wore a zebra striped hair bonnet that always made me laugh. That thing was so raggedy.

"Tramp you might as well move in because you either call me or stop by at the same time every night," she fussed standing with her hand on her hip. She continued,

"Come in. You right on time too, I'm about to spark up."

"Yes, I need to smoke. Girl, you won't believe who walked into Landing Strip," I mentioned while walking inside straight to the smoke room.

"Oh, this about to be good."

She loved to hear about my nightly adventures even though she hated that I danced. The smoke room was like a mini living room with a hunter green loveseat, two end tables, and a forty-inch flat screen smart television. The loveseat turned into a sofa sleeper. She had Bob Marley posters on the wall along with other marijuana-themed stuff. Comfortable on the loveseat she closed the door and handed me the blunt and lighter.

"You need the first few puffs more than I do. Here blaze it up," she encouraged.

I put the fire to the tip of the cigar as it burned evenly before taking a nice, hard drag. With my eyes closed, I held the smoke as long as possible before exhaling. I took a few more pulls then passed it back to her. The effects of the herbs beg to take effect as my eyes felt heavy, yet my entire body was relaxed.

"Queen, my damn father and his deacons walked in tonight as I performed and it was the most disturbing moment. Can you imagine the look on our faces when we discovered each other? I really thought my father was perfect."

"What in the world was he doing there? That is crazy, but your dad is human-- just like everyone else. We all make mistakes."

"True, but that's my daddy! It wasn't a surprise to see Deacon Black, he probably dragged my dad with him. Eli daddy was there too. Deacon Brown was no saint either, but he surprised me too."

"Deacon Black looks like he steps out on his wife. Back in the day, he used to watch the fast tail girls. Anyway, what you gonna do now, quit? It's about time anyway don't you think?"

"Yes, but not yet. The spotlight, money, and men are addicting. Despite what you believe or feel about what I do, it's not a bad job."

"Well, whatever you decide I'll support--because that is what friendship is all about. You want this back?" she extended her arm to me with the small weed roach.

"I'm good. That's some good stuff; I'm mellow as ever now." Suddenly Bad and Boujee played in the background as we both tried to figure out where it came from. The sound came from the zipped compartment of my purse. It was a message from my sister Lauren. I raised an eyebrow. Close to four o'clock in the morning, it scared me.

Dad: Baby girl please forgive me. Can we have dinner to talk?

I glanced at his text as the tears build up before they ran down my cheeks from disappointment. Queen did her best to console me. She was a true definition of a ride or die, we've been friends since middle school and nothing has changed.

"Tia get some rest and wake up fresh, so you can figure out your next moves. I'm taking my ass to bed."

"Thanks, BFF. Love ya, girl." I slept in the smoke room because I was too high to move to the guest room. Later that morning, my eyes popped open from hunger pains so after I used the bathroom and washed my hands and face I went to the kitchen. With a quick browse and search in the fridge, Bingo! I spotted Yoplait strawberry yogurt and Applewood thin sliced bacon. I pulled the items out. Without too much noise, I retrieved a large black skillet from the bottom cabinet and placed it on the stove. Each slice of bacon was lined up in the skillet as the fire slowly sparked making the grease formulate. While that cooked, I enjoyed each spoonful of yogurt until it was gone.

"Damn it smells so good my mouth watering. I hope you cooked me some too!"

"How rude would I be if I told you no? Ha, I'm just playing, of course, I cooked enough for you." Our laughter filled the kitchen as the smell of pork made my stomach jump for joy. Queen came right in headed to the double cabinet, she retrieved a box of Quaker Oatmeal. Six pieces of bacon later I packed up and headed home to regroup. During the drive, I thought about my parents and life in general.

My mother, Connie Wallace was uppity, sarcastic, caring, and a God-fearing woman who had plans for my life. I wasn't having it; being married to a pastor like she had to do with my dad. That was not in my plan. She was able to control my younger sisters, Lauren and Gabrielle, but not me. My rebellious ways are one reason we bumped heads a lot. I'm Tia Wallace, the oldest child and I moved out at eighteen because my mom and I always got into it. The sarcastic comments she tended to make always got to my soul no matter how I tried to ignore them.

My father, Pastor Charles Wallace, was the best parent a girl could ever ask for. Unlike my mother, he actually cared about me and not my screw-ups. He never judged nor brought up things from the past. My dad always made time for my sisters and me no matter what he had to do for the church or congregation. In my eyes, he was the perfect person I knew growing up, at least until the incident.

Did I lose you yet? Let me take yall back to how I first got started dancing in the first place. Queen and I pulled into the lot of the Landing Strip Lounge to go check out Nakia at work. We planned to stay for a good hour, long enough to show our support and get a few laughs. I'd never set foot in a gentlemen's club before. All the stuff from television had me nervous. Before we stepped out the car, she pulled a blunt from her glove compartment. We smoked half of it and I was no longer nervous. I imagined a bunch of drunk horny men falling all over, slurring works, or harassing the dancers.

"I'm ready to see what the hype is all about," Queen stated as we entered dressed in denim skinny jeans, with a nice dressy top that showed just enough cleavage.

Straight to the bar, she ordered two vodka and cranberry juices. It was the exact opposite; the atmosphere was chill, the men kept it cordial, and the drinks were just right. Because it was our first time, I suggested seats close enough to an exit just in case of an emergency. In a relaxed state, the night got more exciting once our girl hit the stage. If anyone told me that a person could swing and work a pole as good as Nakia, I would call him or her a liar. Her ass clowned not to mention all of the men who threw money at her on stage.

I took a sip of my drink as I watched the men whistle and practically drool over the half-naked women. "How awkward do you think it is to be in the spotlight? It's cool in the mirror at home but this is too much."

"I'm not sure but you got a secret admirer over there. The white boy keeps looking this way, so it must be because of you."

"What? Stop playing," I spoke before slowly glancing his way. Sure enough, there he sat with two men. Before I could turn my head from staring, he caught me. *Damn*, I thought as he got up from his seat to approach me.

"Oh, here he comes. What do I do?"

"Talk to him, stop being shy. Remember-- we only live once friend."

A semi-deep voice spoke. I could tell he wasn't a black man. "Excuse me, lovely ladies. I couldn't help but notice you from across the room. Y'all want to join us?"

"Hi. Umm, we actually came to see a friend perform then we plan to leave," I replied without paying attention to the guy who spoke.

"Never mind her, we would love to join you three. It will make the more fun and entertaining," Queen broadcasted.

"Great. I'm Lance by the way," he extended his hand to each of us as he planted a kiss on mine. When we made eye contact a lump formed in my throat. *Damn, a white boy as fine as him, wow.*

"Nice to meet you, I guess."

"Oh, that hurt," he said.

"Oh no! I'm sorry, I didn't mean it like that. It's just...who gets hit on at a strip club? Let's just have fun before I insult you more," I joked.

"No worries sweetheart, I can take anything you throw my way. Is it okay that we join you over here? We got all drinks and singles for the dancers."

"Hell yeah! Y'all come hang with us fine sistas for the night," Queen insisted.

"Cool. Give us a few to switch over."

"Oh my goodness, Queen, he is beyond gorgeous. Did you see those blue eyes? I think I might have to get down with the swirl if his game is right." Five strangers together in a place full of dancers was an unexpected evening that made me want to dance even more. I needed to find out if Lance was a frequent customer or if it was a spare.

While Lance and I got to know each other a little better, Queen and his two friends found a few chicks to make it rain on. I had the best of both worlds with my best friend. She found entertainment long enough for me to chop it up with Lance.

"So, do you frequent this place often or is this just a night with fellas?"

"A night out with the boys to unwind after a long workday. I assume you don't come here often either huh?"

"Nope, just came to support a friend but I'm thinking about working here for a while; something spontaneous to help me come out of my shell."

"In that case, consider me a new and faithful client. No, seriously, there's nothing wrong with living a little--just don't let this job change you. Real talk."

"Wow, advice from a stranger, how nice of you. My acquaintance convinced me to try it just to help make some extra money. She insisted my pole skills had improved well enough to perform on stage."

"Not being a pervert, but I would undeniably be your favorite client. My job keeps me busy and the best part about the night is unwinding. I'd rather do that with you anytime possible even if it meant coming here twice a week."

"You are such a charming man that obviously was taught how to flatter a woman. I must admit, this is weird yet enjoyable. I've honestly had a good time chatting."

"This is embarrassing but you never told me your name. We've had this wonderful connection, but I don't know your name."

"Ha, how funny is that. I'm Tia. When you came up to my friend and me it was a surprise. Never thought a man would be interested; people come to see the dancers."

"I'm here to unwind from the workday and see a little action from the girls. That was until I saw you, now I'd rather enjoy your company and ignore the world. A pretty laid-back person, I like to meet like-minded people who like to work hard and play hard. From the short time we've sat here, I've felt nothing but good vibes."

"Same here, I work with freshman students three to four days a week; all I do is work. Tonight, is out of my element...but it's been an interesting night, to say the least. All of a sudden, Juicy J "Bandz a Make Her Dance" played through the sound system. That song made everyone move and bounce their body; it was like an anthem song in a place like this. I'd never saw so many different shades and shapes of asses in my life.

"Damn, these women know how to move their body, umm," Lance said just as hypnotized as me. No disrespect but, I bet you can move that attractive body of yours too."

"Oh, you have no idea how hard it is not to get up and dance right now."

"What's stopping you from dancing? I would love to see you in action. You can't be shy if you plan to work here, so let me be your first customer. Let me help you get used to performing."

"Damn this white boy talking a good game and I sure didn't mind twirling my ass for him. But will that make me look easy?" I wondered to myself as he sat back undressing me with his button blue eyes. I looked around before I got up and let the music control my body. My confidence level was at a ten, so I didn't care who watched or what they thought. In that instance the fears left my body and mind, Lance pulled out his money and politely tucked bills along the waistline of my jeans. I didn't want to feel insulted because that was how money was made in this type of establishment.

When the song went off, I took a seat next to him removing each bill he placed on me. To my surprise, he had stuffed one thousand dollars in big face one hundreds. If he was serious about being a main client, then I would be able to save enough money in no time. It wasn't until closing time, I realized how much fun I had. That night was the first of many nights of my dancing career.

The five of us reconnected and walked out of the door together, as if we all came together as friends. The swagger Lance had was hard to deny because that man made me want to jump his bones in the back of my car. I looked him wanting to know more and possibly see him again. "Aye, so thank you for tonight even though you are a complete stranger. Tonight, I learned not to judge a book by its cover and the fact that milk in my coffee might be worth a try."

"Can I call or text you beautiful? There is no way I can go without ever seeing you again; even it's only a friendship you want."

"Sure, let's swap phones." We entered each other's number and saved them before switching back. I saved my number under the name Nubian Queen, so he knew who I was. Around him, it seemed like time stood still. In reality, Queen was yelling for me to get my ass in the car. I laughed out loud right before Lance took my hand and kissed it-- the same way he greeted me earlier.

"Be sweet my Nubian Queen. Until next time...take care of yourself, baby!"

Inside, we pulled off and I told my friend everything that happened as she drove back to her home; which only took forty minutes. When we exited her car and walked towards the front entrance, my stomach growled so loud-- it startled me.

"Best Frand, you should put two pizzas in the oven-- I'm hungry as a hostage. Girl, I had so much fun and even made a thousand bucks. Imagine if I actually worked there."

"Bih! I saw you all cozy with old boy, he was so into you-- it was just sad. You had that man in love. Be careful; you know they ass get crazily obsessed. Naw, I'm just playing."

"No, you not. Girl, he was too laid back and down to earth. Our vibe was synced or something. Lance has his own type of swag that makes me want to get to know him, but if I get the job at the club; it will be weird."

"That will be your way to indirectly interrogate him and make money."

"He would be a good friend to hang with from time to time, but it's too early for that. Aye, is the pizza brown yet? My stomach about to go nuts."

"Almost fat girl! Can you get us something to drink from the refrigerator? Grab me a Dr. Pepper please."

"Gotcha," Tia said as she put two Dr. Peppers on the counter while I took the pizzas from the oven. Because we were so hungry Tia took the mushroom and sausage and I ate the pepperoni and pineapple. Once the food disappeared, we moved to the smoking room. It was lights out afterwards.

* * *

My first night in a gentleman's club wasn't anything I expected, nor did I think of meeting a guy. The next evening, Queen came to my house for a few hours as we smoked, laughed and watched every movie we could think of that had strippers in it. I had a notebook taking notes like it was a homework assignment. Of course, we watched Player's Club: one of the most quoted movies of all time. Halfway through, Queen suddenly turned to me and said, "Aye, when you start working; make that money girl, but don't let it make you."

Laughter was my response even though I know what she said was nothing but the truth. Dancing wasn't something every woman could do or had a choice in doing when bills needed to be paid. Suddenly it dawned on me, what if I didn't have what it takes to do the job? There was fifty percent doubt but regardless, Nakia believed in my skills so there was no reason to not believe in myself.

"Aye, I should get a pole installed," I suggested joking as I sat up on the light gray sectional.

"Ooh girl you are a hot mess, but I will enjoy it if you do. Aye. You know what I was thinking? We should take another class; advanced this time."

"Go online to look it up, but if I get this job working with Nakia; I might not have time. Check it out and let me know what is offered." We spent the rest of the time chilling, watching movies and blowing-- a regular part of our schedule.

Two weeks later, I started my gig as a dancer. It was a Saturday and Nakia had me meet her downtown for an audition she set up with the owner. Not expecting to do a full routine, I planned on using the techniques I learned from Miss Pole classes, with a twist of impromptu. The tall beauty queen looking woman sat ready to be impressed. She observed me from head to toe as if she liked what she saw. My thoughts wondered if she was straight or bisexual. Either way--it didn't bother me.

"Hi, I'm Tia," I extended my hand, but she just looked at me. Her rudeness was the first sign this was a bad idea.

"I'm Chastity. Don't get the wrong impression dear. This place is for those with thick skin and sex appeal. You definitely have that, but I need to know if you can really do this job. What do you do for a living?"

"I teach freshman students at a community college so trust I have thick skin. Don't judge this book by its cover because I'm sure this job would be no different. I deal with horny eighteen-year-olds and snotty girls three days a week. How about I do my performance then you make your call."

Her face displayed a look of interest once she realized I wasn't that quiet. She shook her head in agreement as her hand motioned for Nakia to assist me. In a smaller area of the club, the music from my cell phone played loud enough to dance to. Before walking on the stage, I pulled the dress over my head and laid it in a chair. With shorts and a tank top on, I was ready to prove myself. With a head nod, Nakia started the music. Partition by Beyoncé played as my body began to feel the beat. Soon the shyness faded, and I twirled on that pole like a professional. Her music made me feel fierce as if I was a part of her entourage. Like an alter ego, I turned into someone else as my body moved seductively giving the rude woman what she wanted.

When I finished it stunned me that I actually performed. Nervous, yet excited, I breathed heavily--the adrenaline pumping. With no type of emotion or sign if she liked my performance, I moved closer to the table and slipped my dress back on.

"I like it! You are really natural for this. You can start tonight, Tia. Umm, you know what? Your name is Coco; I like that better," Chastity commented. She sat at a table surrounded by money with a joint in her mouth. "Wow. Thank you!"

"Go with Nakia so she can show you the ropes. She will help you until needed. Alright now leave me, I got money to count."

Eager to assist, Nakia said, "We need to go find you a few pieces to wear, get your nails done, and of courses heels. Coco, you made one hell of an impression on Boss Lady because she usually does not hire too fast. Girl, you bout to make some bread. Mark my words."

"Girl what if I choke tonight and embarrass the hell out of myself?"

"Think positive! Think about the money! Worst case scenario, drink a shot or two.

It will help loosen you a bit. Now come on so we can shop, eat, and then nap. "We headed for the door into the lot when I realized my purse and phone was locked in my trunk.

"Aye I need to grab my purse from the car right fast," I shouted to her. She waited for me to grab it then I got inside her car ready to shop. During the entire time together, we talked about how to choose clients, tips, and the other working girls.

"What if I just watch tonight for last minute notes and observations, then start Monday night. I'm a professor remember?"

"You pick the days you work so if that makes you more at ease, fine. Just make sure to let Boss Lady know your plans."

"You need to establish a regular clientele with the customers. You gotta tip well in order to gain good service with the bartender, DJ, and the cocktail waitresses. The first few times you might not make enough bread to take home, but the way you show out, I don't know."

"How do I know if the client has the money or just trying to luck up on a free dance?"

"Make his ass show you the money. If you get a bad feeling or something you can say no thank you. Oh yeah, some other words of advice; chicks will smile in your face so watch ya back. If you become good enough to hit up wallets before the others, they will get jealous."

"Wow this is information overload, but I'm glad to know what to expect first hand. Tell me some more stuff on how the life is. How long do most girls last?" We spent two hours together as if we knew each other for years. I bought a few items and she returned me to my car. Later that night, I watched the girls put in work ready for my turn.

Two nights later, it was my time to show off the talents that got me hired. I sat at my vanity wearing a pink lace sheer bodysuit. Looking in the mirror at how striking I was, Nakia signaled that it was time to hit the floor. Behind her, I followed observing the crowd. As a professor, it should've been easy to do this job but in the moment of being half naked in a lounge--my nerves kicked in. Within the first two hours, my level of comfort was low. A few clients who gave me a chance were able to tell it was my first night. Just when I got discouraged, a familiar face appeared, Lance. Our last encounter took place in this building. He was feeling me last time. His presence helped me relax enough to get through my shift.

Being the first night I wasn't sure if it was for me but wanted to stick it out for a few months. Getting home late at night was one of the biggest things to adjust to besides approaching men for dances. I dropped everything by the door and sat on my sofa sectional. I expected the job to be like the movie Player's Club, but it wasn't; thank goodness. Instead, the women seemed to work well together and the men weren't rowdy.

All my body craved for was warm water and illicit smoke after the first night of dancing. In the shower I washed with Caress Adore Forever body wash. It smelled so good and released a perfume scent lasting up to twelve hours. Feeling like a new woman, it was amazing what water and smell good soap could do. In my nightwear, I got in the bed with my smoke by the bedside. Just as I lit the blunt, Queen called, as if she smelled it.

"Girl, I'm glad we took that class because some of my muscles not as sore as I thought. But let me tell you, dancing is a complete workout from the beginning to the end. I'm going to need a set workout schedule and diet starting tomorrow.

"I hope you will be able to come with me to get my nails done every two weeks. Aye, they also gave me a gym membership at Planet Fitness to keep my body in shape."

"You do that anyway now you can do it on their dime. What was it like? You can't leave out any details either."

"Most of the girls been dancing for at least two years or more and each one had their own advice to give me. Oh, and the owner, Chastity, is cool as hell and she blows too. Her rudeness turned out to be just the way she appeared. She lit a joint during my audition. Anyway, it was just like the night we visited."

"How were the men? Any freaks or weird ones come your way?"

"A mixture of regular looking dudes like the night we went. Speaking of, white chocolate stopped in. Dude, Lance should be married to some lily-white girl, yet his interest is in me."

"Oh Lawd! my best friend about to catch jungle fever. Mrs. Wallace would have a fit to see you with a man she didn't pick."

"We shall see what happens, but until then a sista will remain single. Besides, no fraternizing. Ha, her crazy ass probably would fall to the floor, with her melodramatic self."

"Yeah, we will see. He too fine to ignore girl. If things move forward it's because of your first-time meeting as customers. Shouldn't be a fraternizing issue."

"You too much."

"Alright girl, I gotta grade papers and take my butt to bed. Chat with you tomorrow. Peace out!"

"Holla Black," Queen said before the call dropped.

With a smile plastered on my face as if someone could see it, my thoughts drifted to the white man. It felt wrong to like him given my ancestors were slaves, but he wasn't to blame for the actions of stupid racists. Lance appeared different from typical guys I tended to meet. He didn't try to impress me as much as he was just himself the entire time. His willingness to stuff big face money down my pants for conversation was a good vibe. I felt the need to entertain him more and in return gain a friendship or courtship; whichever came first.

My plan to grade papers ended up not happening because I got too stoned. My eyes were so heavy and low, all I could do was lay still and let the effects wear off. That batch of smoke was almost like drinking and having a hangover afterward. Instead, thoughts of Lance resurfaced which got me slightly hot and bothered. I imagined a night of wild passionate sex with him. From our encounters with one another, I assumed his experience in the bedroom was above average but not to the point that he'd slept with numerous women. Sex was a sin, but it was something I craved and fought every day. Nighttime was the worst, but a little Porn Hub and Mary Jane did the trick.

CHAPTER 4

onnie Wallace
    Doing laundry on a Saturday was something that helped me past the time and gain Fitbit points all in one. In the midst of emptying the clothes from the hamper, a white piece of paper fell to the floor. I bent over to pick it up, glancing at it. My eyes focused on the date and time stamp. I'd never heard of the place on the receipt. I snatched my pink HP laptop and took a seat in the white chair at the oversized Calcutta marble counter island. I grabbed a bottle of Sutter Home White Zinfandel. A glass of wine in the middle of the day wasn't a sin.

That receipt nagged at me until the voice in my mind told me to check out the place. I Google the name of the place, and it surprised me to find out it was a gentlemen's club. Stunned, I put my hand over my mouth embarrassed. What was I not doing in the bedroom to make my husband go to a place he shouldn't have? I wondered, reflecting on our marriage.

Minutes later, I called my good girlfriend, Juanita for some womanly advice. With a few taps of a finger the phone was on speaker as I waited for an answer. Juanita was my partner in crime whenever it was time to investigate.

"Hi, Lady Wallace," her voice projected through the phone."

"You are too much Nita girl! What are you doing?"

"Chile, I just watched Y&R and the drama never stops! Monday can't come fast enough. Anyway, what's up?"

"I'm in the kitchen enjoying a glass of wine while I wait for the washing machine to stop. That brings me to the reason of my call," I paused long enough to take a sip before I went on.

"Oh, snap do I need a glass too?"

"It's not that deep, but if you feel the need, go right ahead. Anyway, in the midst of sorting clothes, and a receipt fell from Charles' pocket. Girl, he might be stepping out on me. I'm not sure though because there is no hardcore proof."

"Don't go blaming yourself friend, men always find a way to mess stuff up. You do enough with the church and running a home."

"True as that may be, why go there instead of coming to me about his issue? He is the main one who preached about honesty."

"Well think about how he has been acting or strange things you've noticed lately. Does anything come to mind? If not, it could be innocent."

"Nita for years Charles and I have lived together, there hasn't been anything suspicious. My woman's intuition would've given me a sign, but there is nothing. Why does this bother me so much?"

"I'm not sure. Maybe it's nothing. Maybe he's connected to something that makes him innocent. Just investigate a bit more but don't say anything to him yet," Juanita advised.

"I'll put it on the back burner for now but trust me; I will continue to investigate," I said with raised eyebrows as if she could see me through the phone. "You know what? We should go check out the place right now."

"Connie, you know I'm not trying to get into your marital affairs but..."

"But nothing! You are coming to pick me up in the next twenty minutes. I'm about to switch the clothes from washer to dryer. See you soon friend," I insisted not giving her a chance to say no.

"Damn girl. Oh I mean dang. See you soon," she joked.

Dressed down in a plain black short sleeve summer dress, I slipped on a half-length blue jean jacket. A half-hour later, Juanita pulled up outside in her two-door maroon Ford Focus with tinted windows. She was ready to play eye spy with me. The moment my seatbelt clicked she drove off.

"What's our plan, sista?"

"I just want to see the place in person, not trying to start trouble or disclose my identity. Huh, I'm sure glad you have tinted windows; can't have people seeing my face."

"You a mess, Connie."

We pulled into a parking lot and parked in front of a building with two big red lips plastered on each side of it. I felt my face frown, but quickly adjusted. I tried to understand why men wasted money and time on a place like it.

"Now what?" Juanita asked as she looked around the lot.

"We go home. I have laundry to finish and dinner to prep. Just needed to see the place in person you know. I'll give you gas money if that's what you're worried about."

"Girl get out of your feelings, I don't need gas money but a plate of whatever you cooking, will be fine by me," she tilted her head with a big smile then laughed. Her unique laugh made us both bust in giggles hysterically. I'd had wine, I didn't know what her excuse was. She put the gear in drive and peeled out and back to the street. With my head back against the headrest, I enjoyed the ride back home as a calm sensation flowed through my body. The ride back home felt quicker than it did going to the place. Juanita drove into our long turn around driveway parking close to the front door. No cars parked in front of the two-car garage, there was time to cook and let Juanita take a plate by the time my girls made it home.

Walking up the five concrete stairs, I inserted my key in to unlock the door as we walked in. We were tired as if we had really just done something. I laid my keys on the table in the foyer and walked towards the kitchen. Juanita followed behind me taking her shades off, setting them on the counter with her purse. It didn't take her long to settle in and get comfortable.

"Help yourself to whatever," I stated as I went to the sink to wash my hands. Then I turned on the 19-inch flat screen television for us while I gathered the necessary items needed to prepare the meal. Moving around the kitchen was a breeze as it took me no time to brown the meat, boil the pasta shells. The process didn't take me long that was the joy in easy meals.

An hour later, Juanita and I had eaten. She left, and I folded and put away the laundry. Gabby and Lauren arrived home and ate but went back to their rooms. I chatted with each about their day then went to my bedroom for a nice warm shower and nightly reading. By nightfall, Charles made it home fussing about the deacons, per usual. With my face in my book, I was all hot and bothered from the novel. I wanted him to get naked and come give me some of his polish sausage. My concern about him cheating was out of my head as if the thought never crossed my mind. Fresh and freaky I needed him, wanted him, to give me some good loving. While he showered I, moved from my rocking chair to the bed, in position ready to be pleased.

When I felt his warm body slide under the cover, I instantly felt myself get moist. He still gave me that feeling after years of being together. Reading had my mind in the gutter. It was okay, sex wasn't a sin especially with my husband. His gentle touch made me open up like a flower in the blooming phase. Moments like this make me feel stupid I had Juanita driving around town. It was silly of me to believe my husband would cheat on me. So to redeem myself, I decided to give Charles some oral sex. Performing that act was only for special occasions but that particular night counted. I turned to face him with a grin while I stroked his salt-n-pepper hair

"Baby, do you feel like fooling around? That book has me in a playful mood if you catch my drift."

"How playful you trying to be? I need to be sleep in an hour but I'm willing to have a little bedtime fun."

"Good. Take off your bottoms," I demanded. Once he was bare underneath, I positioned myself and gripped his meat placing inside my mouth. His lite moans let me know he enjoyed it, but he sat up in the middle of my performance.

"Wow, what did I do to deserve this type of treatment? This only happens on special nights. Wait, what did-," his words became moans as my tongue did circles around the tip and head of his manhood. In a pleasurable manner, my mouth went into overtime until he yelled out.

"STOP! Get on top, I wanna feel you--all of you. I'm at my peak baby."

I did as he asked and slid down on his pole, without hesitation, until he was completely inside of me. The union of our bodies, the rhythm of my hips in motion with his, felt so right. Charles loved me on top; said he could feel my every move in that position. Back and forth, up and down, we continued as our speed increased. Minutes later, he let out a deep grunt and released his soldiers. I did the same as I climbed off top to stretch my legs. A quick bathroom and wash up break did me justice, then I cuddled under my papa bear. Whenever he wrapped his arms around me I felt so safe and secure, like we were meant to be together. It was the type of moment I savored, never wanted it to end. Charles worked so hard and poured his life into the church, anytime we were alone together, I cherished. Heavy eyelids and the sandman swept me into a calm sleep until the next morning. I woke and prepped for Sunday service like normal.

CHAPTER 5

*C*onnie Wallace

Like any other member of the congregation, I wasn't perfect. I too was a sinner, but repented and prayed to be a better person each day. The Book of Proverbs guided me in that journey. The path of wisdom was a true blessing; thankful for every chance to grow wiser. After breakfast, I applied a touch-up coat of Mac Lipstick. Smoked purple was cute and classy with my floral knee-length pencil dress and accessories. The dress displayed my figure in a classy way. At my age the curves were still visible, so I sure wasn't shame to flaunt them.

The last one to come out of the house, I got in the truck. We arrived at the church in less than thirty minutes. Charles drove into the church parking lot and parked in his reserved space. Lauren and Gabby exited the vehicle the moment the engine shut off. Nowadays these teenagers acted as if it would kill them to disconnect from the wireless world long enough to spend a few hours in the Lord's house. Charles drove quietly while I got on Lauren's case about having her iPhone.

"Lauren please don't think you are slick child. Gimme that phone, now."

"Dang Mama, why you always treating me like a kid? Technically I'm grown, so it's not fair that I can't hold onto my phone."

"Girl please, don't make me lose my tongue before the service even starts. We are about to go inside and prep for service. Why do you need this darn thing anyway? The purpose of attending church is to hear the word of God from your father, repent for our sins, and pray. You will get your phone when church is over."

"But..."

I put my hand up to stop her. "Not one more word Lauren Nicole Wallace." She sucked her teeth in without uttering another peep. When I called any of my girls by their entire name, it was a warning to hush with the flip lip.

Charles and Gabby left us to it as they walked inside to get thing set-up. Lauren was a good child, however, she had some of her big sister's attitude ways that got under my skin. We strolled inside the building to set-up. As the parent of three daughters, my faith was constantly tested by the two oldest.

Despite the headache, my love for them never changed; even when I wanted to lay hands on them. The gift to speak was more of a curse than a blessing for Tia. She back talked to me as a teenager saying stuff to make me tick. Her method was to shoot low blows that would me make step out of character. Even as an adult she never thought before she spoke, a reason we could never be cordial at dinner. At times I wondered where things went wrong with her. *Faith without works* was going to be very difficult if she refused to work.

While the girls were upstairs in the sanctuary, I stood in the doorway of our office as Charles slipped on his collar and robe. He was the most handsome man. My husband and I had a long history, one that had sustained for over twenty years. Marriage was a wonderful thing, but had its challenges like any other relationship. Forced to marry Charles by mother, she never asked how it made me feel because she only cared for herself. Before Charles, there was my high school sweetheart, Joseph, the man I wanted to wed. Our hopes and dreams cut short to fulfill the self-satisfying mother from hell. Over time we grew to love each other as husband and wife.

"I'm ready," Charles indicated as he turned towards me. We held hands and prayed together before heading upstairs. I greeted each person as they entered the doors.

"Good morning! Welcome to Calvary," my words repeated as the people flocked inside. Even though it was summer time, our numbers were decent as usual. We weren't a big-time megachurch, however, we had a constant number in attendance. Close to two hundred made it their business to hear my husband. The church bells began to ring, which was indication service would start momentarily.

When my head raised up I noticed Ms. Dale in a two-tone Pink Set by Donna Vinci. *Oh my, here come this with this fake smile plastered on her face. She can't stand my guts and the feeling is mutual,* I thought as she approached me. Being the bigger person, I returned the smirk the minute we were face to face. "Good morning Ms. Dale, you are looking radiant today. Come right on in." Really, I wanted to tell her all that pink made me sick. She would have been better off with a less vibrant color. It was hard to maintain a smile without chuckling at my thoughts.

"Good morning, First Lady Wallace," she spoke on her way past me.

I turned my attention to Gabrielle, who handed everyone a fan along with a hymnbook as the ushers seated newcomers. My baby was such a beautiful young woman who would be the one to continue the family legacy. She had many of her father's qualities, which lead me to believe she was the chosen one. I've never seen a child so obedient, loving, and compassionate.

As the last crowd of people entered the building, we closed the doors and encouraged folks to sit so the service could proceed. I took my place in the front pew next to Juanita as Gabby joined me. Juanita was a good girlfriend of mine for almost six years now. We shared the same sense of humor and love for the soap opera, Young & The Restless. Over the years, we had grown close like sisters.

My eyes quickly scanned for Lauren before my focus went back up to the front. Then sounds of the drums and piano served as cue for the choir who marched down the aisle in their blue robes. As they marched and sang "Heaven" by Mary Mary, their sound and rhythm woke the church up. Charles instructed everyone to open their hymn books to page seventy-nine to join.

I admired my husband as he stood before the people each week doing what he called, 'spreading the word'. No doubt his gift was in ministry, but I'm sure attending strip clubs weren't part of ministry. A receipt fell from his pocket for a non-alcoholic beer at some place called Landing Strip Lounge. Without more knowledge, my suspicions took a back burner for the time being. As the First Lady, I had an image to uphold and a role to play. His careless actions of going into a filthy place like that could jeopardize all we've worked. With being in the spotlight, I couldn't afford to make mistakes for all to see. My mom and dad instilled in me the importance of responsibility and serving the people.

His deep strong masculine voice projected through the microphone clipped to his robe. When the choir took position in front of their seats, he instructed everyone bow heads for prayer. "Heavenly Father, we thank You for the blessings You have provided to us. Thank you for the blessing to breathe and gather to worship You. You are worthy of our praise. Amen!"

"Amen!" I shouted along with the others as he continued.

"Welcome to Calvary all who are visiting for the first time. Enjoy the service and fellowship that follows afterward. We will now hear the first reading from Sister Daniels." Sister Daniels pranced up front with her hand out for the mic. My focus diverted down memory lane while she stood before the church to read.

Married at age twenty-three was something my mother wanted more than I did. In time my love for him grew, and he became my best friend. Before I was appointed to be the lady of the church, my interest in culinary school almost became a reality. I dreamed of having a televised cooking show and writing cooking books--but God had something in store for me to do. I was stubborn to the idea of children early in my marriage. I gave in by the time I turned thirty-three, and got pregnant with Tia. As the eldest, she was a free-spirited young lady that didn't like to follow the rules.

Once Charles became an ordained pastor, life changed for the better as our family grew from three to five. Obviously, my sex game kept him, but over the years the activity declined. Our sex life suffered because of his on the go schedule all the time. Nevertheless, I gave up the goods as much as he is around. So, when I found a receipt from Landing Strip Lounge; imagine my concern. It puzzled me, yet a word never left my lips, nor did he even suspect anything. My investigation into the matter officially began that moment. Any woman in my position understood my position. I be darned if my husband is caught in a scandal; our family image was too important.

After the sermon, he broke out singing "We've Come This Far by Faith" as he wiped the sweat from his forehead then waved his hand. "C'mon choir, help sing this song now."

That song always made me feel highly favored as I stood to my feet, clapped my hands and sang along. Each week, the choir provided soulful sounds for worship that kept the people praising his holy name. Regardless of not being televised like the mega-churches, Calvary was a well-known church with potential to become prominent for years. It was my duty to make it happen, but Deacon Black was the roadblock who made it tough. Nevertheless, as James 2:14-26 stated, "Faith without work is dead," so it was my duty to work. In the next five years, it was my plan to get Charles elected Regional Minister of Wisconsin. It's not as if we didn't deserve it for the leadership and dedication we put into our church home. Unaware, Charles didn't know about my low key plan but would soon figure it out when we traveled to Atlanta in October.

"Amen!" I shouted again as the choir had slowly ended the song by humming.

"Congregation, let's join hands and bow our heads in prayer. Let us give thanks for thee who has given us so much. Let's pray for the sick and addicted. We all need it. Deacon Black, lead us will you, please." Everyone locked hands with bowed heads to silently pray for those in need. The choir closed out with one last song of praise. Charles gave the benediction and dismissed the congregation.

* * *

FINALLY, home, the first thing I did was change out of my church clothes into loose fitting jogging suit. Charles followed me to our room to do the same. Whenever his schedule permitted, he liked to go to his man cave for a while until dinner was done. I went back downstairs, washed my hands and began to prep the food.

My family requested fried catfish, spaghetti, and garlic bread. To keep me, company I turned on the television to watch Saturday Night Live. Alec Baldwin did one heck of a job impersonating Donald Trump. While I listened and laughed, I seasoned then coated the fish in cornmeal placing each piece in a pan until the grease was hot enough. The ground turkey had browned and been drained already. Once the water came to a nice boil, I added the noodles and placed the fish in the sizzling grease. Finally, I preheat the oven when the fish was close to done. Like a creature of habit, my husband appeared just as I set the table. As a family, Charles blessed the food and we blessed our stomachs.

After dinner, we sat in the family room to watch the television show, Greenleaf. The show aired on Wednesday nights, but we set the DVR to record it. It was a way for us to gather together to enjoy each other's company. During this time no cell phone, laptops, or any other device were allowed. Too many families were divided because of the intrusion of technology. The girls didn't mind because the show was too good not to pay attention. The Greenleaf family was worse than ours not to mention all of the secrets amongst them. However, the mother and daughter relationship between Lady Mae and Grace was similar to Connie and Tia.

On the beige L-shaped couch Connie sat with her legs across my lap as I massaged her feet. I glared at her periodically when scenes with the mother and daughter happened. It was like having those two characters in my home whenever Tia paid us a visit. It had been two weeks since Tia came over for dinner and it bothered me a lot. I missed her and wished she would stop avoiding me. Tia used to love to hang around me. I was her role model--the man who would always love her unconditionally.

Daydreaming, Connie's voice snapped me back to the television. "I'm sorry baby, what did you say?"

"I can't stand Mack dirty self. I'm going to bed on that note. Good night kids," she said as she made her way up the staircase. "Good night girls. Daddy loves you. I'm going to bed now." The finale was great, made me do some thinking about the sermon. I climbed the stairs, entered the bedroom and climbed in bed to cuddle with Connie until I drifted off.

CHAPTER 6

Pastor Charles Wallace

"Can I get an Amen? I said, can I get an Amen up in here church! Good morning and welcome to the house of the Lord. Let's give the choir one more hand, whew! Hallelujah. That was a beautiful song choir," I stated as I stood at the pulpit glancing around the church. Folks were waving their fans, hands, and bibles in the air as they stood on their feet. Their reactions made it easy for me to transition into the sermon of the day. Once the noise faded and the silence settled in, I continued.

"Ushers, please rest your feet while I preach for y'all. I want to talk about something that has troubled my spirit. Last week an incident occurred in front of me at the hospital that left me mind-bottled. Two young people were in what looked like a deep conversation. One was the aggressor and the other remained calmed." I paused to sip my water quenching my thirst before I continued on. "Suddenly, the calm one jumped up and threw the Styrofoam cup with coffee in the face of the aggressor. I prayed the coffee didn't burn the person's face. I'm telling you this to say...No one can steal your joy without your permission so don't let them! You are not responsible for the way they act."

"Preach!" a woman from the back shouted.

"Don't give them the satisfaction by stepping out of your character; that is what they want. Tell that devil to get back, walk away before you stoop to their level. Every action doesn't deserve a reaction."

"Amen Pastor!" Ms. Jackson shouted as she sat with the other elders.

"Church let me ask you a question. How many of you are cooking Sunday dinner for your family?" I scanned and saw a few hands raise up in the air.

"Okay, when you leave here, it's possible you will need to make a grocery store run for some last minute items. If you go to the meat section and see there are only two ham hocks left and a lady has her eye on them, don't go fighting each other for it. I don't want to turn on the news and see any of you tossed in jail for fighting over a piece of meat. Maybe it was the Lord's ways of saying you don't need that pork." A few folks chuckled because they knew where I was coming from. I continued, "In all seriousness folks, my point is: no matter the situation or location, remain humbled."

Standing behind the pulpit, I felt like a fraud--a person who didn't deserve to preach to the congregation. It was difficult getting through the sermon. It was just two days ago my feet set foot in a strip club. Why was it that Deacon Black and Deacon Brown could just sit with a clear conscious? After all, it was Deacon Black who tricked me into going in the first place. He was a wolf in sheep clothing who had to be watched like a hawk. His deception was the very reason I refused to give that proposal a second look. His down low craving to be pastor always made me wonder about the hidden agenda he had.

With my attention turned to my daughter, I couldn't help but notice Lauren and Azriah all smiles with each other. That little nappy headed boy was always sniffing around her. I prayed he was nothing like his devilish father. The last thing we needed was those two getting serious or worse. Lauren seemed to really like him though, which made it difficult to bite my tongue about him when she was around. I wrapped up the sermon as the spirit lead me in song followed by the choir who stood to their feet to sing. "We've Come This Far by Faith," was one of my favorite hymns because it was a testimony to my life. It was by faith and prayer that I lead my people and minister His word. Without another word, I just waved my hand and let the music take hold of my body.

The sounds of shouting, tambourines, and praise filled the space from the three hundred members. With collection plates circling around, the gift of giving tended to double when the music moved the crowd. Unlike other churches, our collection plate only went around twice: during the beginning and then towards the end before communion. Deacon Black stood from his seat and by my side as we waited for the two children who served as acolytes. One child carried the money, while the other carried the bread and grape juice; which served as the body and blood of Jesus.

I held the items up and sang "Every day is Thanksgiving" in preparation for the Lord's Supper. Deacon Black and I prayed at the altar with our backs faced to the members. I turned to page thirty-five in my book and gave it to him to hold for me. We then turned to face my brothers and sisters in Christ as I recited Matthew 26: 26-28 "Jesus took bread, gave thanks and broke it saying, take and eat; this is my body. Then he took the cup, gave thanks, saying this is my blood shed for you and for all people. Drink from this for the forgiveness of your sins."

The deacons and I got into position to serve each person who set foot in front of us. The number of people out outnumbered the amount of bread left so we switched to wafers. When we finished each attendee had been served. It pleased me to see so many folks young and old in worship. Again, I turned to face front to lead us all in prayer.

"Let us join hands for the Lord's Prayer. Our Father which art in Heaven, hallowed be your name. Thy kingdom come, thy will be done, on earth as it is in Heaven. Give us this day our daily bread, and forgive us our trespasses, as we forgive those who trespass against us. And lead us not into temptation, but deliver us from evil. For thine is the kingdom, the power, and the glory, forever and ever. Amen."

The choir stood to their feet to sing *Step Aside*, which was one of my favorite songs of all time. When they finished, I proceeded with a closing prayer and the benediction. A few people came up afterward to shake my hand for a great service. That was a reward worth smiling about. My wife approached me with extended arms for a hug. "Honey you were great and the choir--oh my how I love their sound!" Connie exclaimed.

"Thank you, baby."

"Well, I will head down to the office. See you in a few." Connie carried the collection plates in the front of her.

"Okie dokie," I answered taking off my robe to place it on the hook. Reflecting on the morning, a knock on the door caught my attention. When I turned around it was a young man who looked to be no more than twenty. His white t-shirt wasn't so white and his hair hadn't been cut in months. It was evident he had fallen on tough times so without hesitation, I invited him to take a seat.

"How can I help you today, young man?"

"Well sir, I've been down on my luck lately and the church is my last resort. My girlfriend took my car, all of my money, and left me with a pot of spaghetti. For the past week, I've tried to get a job, but no one is willing to give me a chance."

"Wow that is awful to hear son, I'm sorry it happened to you. What type of job skills do you possess? What is your name?"

"Oh sorry, I'm James. I'm good with my hands. I can fix almost anything you put in front of me honestly."

"Umm... Let me see what I can do for you, but it won't be anything permanent. For now, I can offer you a free meal downstairs in the fellowship hall along with a few bus tickets. I want you to come back here on Wednesday evening at six for Men's Ministry. This is help you connect with a few good men who could potentially find you steady employment."

"Oh, that would help me out so much Pastor Wallace. Thank you so much, sir. This has to be the worst month I've been through. To be frank, my faith isn't as strong, and I need prayer. Can you pray for me?"

"Absolutely, we can pray together right now too if you want." It was hard to see one of God's children at a low point in life, hurt, lost, and in need of guidance. I held out my hand palm up and waited for him to take hold of mine. We closed our eyes and bowed our heads for a quick word with God.

"Yes."

"Father, thank you for the many blessings You provide. You are mighty and worthy to be praised. Lord as I sit here with James, we ask for courage, strength, and for faith that the storm won't last forever. Help this young man understand that blessings come in many forms; not just in a financial or materialistic way. Give James hope to keep pushing forward. I ask that You watch over him, guide him, and lead him. In Your name, we pray. Amen."

"Amen. Thank you again, Pastor."

"Anytime. Come on, let's go downstairs for some lunch. I will make sure you get an extra plate to go.

Immediately after the church was cleaned and cleared out, my family and I departed home. Sunday evenings usually entailed downtime until dinner. Connie and I headed to our room to change into comfortable clothing.

Unsure if Tia would attend, I sent her a quick text message, but she ignored it. Unaware of how much longer she would avoid me something had to give.

"Connie, I will be in the study until the food is done. Call me or have one of the girls come get me."

CHAPTER 7

*L*auren Wallace
    Sunday mornings in our household meant you woke up to Yolanda Adams or Tamela Mann blasting through the surround sound speakers the house. In bed, wide awake with my phone in hand, it was a matter of time before my mom busted through the door. Later, she appeared like only she did--chipper with a grin on her face. I swear my mother was a little weird at times.

"Lauren. Good morning my dear daughter! This is the day the Lord has made; let us rejoice and be glad in it. It's time to get up and get ready to praise our Father God."

"Morning mama. I've been awake for a while. Now, I'm literally about to get up." I sat up, yawned, and rubbed my eyes while she stood inches from me.

"Good, be downstairs on time for breakfast."

"Yes, ma'am."

The moment she closed the door behind her, I plopped back on the bed for a few more minutes. Then I made the bed and rushed to shower. A sundress was my preferred outfit, but it was not an option, so I snatched a Nude and Navy flare dress off the hanger. It was a cute dress; simple yet stylish and appropriate for church.

Gabby was already at the table eating by the time my father and I got to the kitchen. My mom placed two medium pancakes, a fried egg, and Tennessee Pride Sausage patties on the plate. Breakfast was the most important meal of the day, especially on Sunday. We never made it home before two in the afternoon. Church was entertaining yet boring at times, so having my iPhone was an enjoyable distraction.

Despite the fact my mother grilled me about my cell phone in church, I did enjoy service. The sound of the choir singing, the tambourines, and the joyous echoes of the congregation in fellowship filled Calvary Christian Life Baptist Church. I sat in the third pew while my mom and little sister Gabby sat in the first one. My father sat alongside the deacons up front behind the pulpit. The choir's song selection *"God is trying to tell you something"* had everyone shouting and praising the Lord.

It was always that one choir member who thought her voice was better than the others. Ms. Thomas was a soprano, so she thought her voice was popping; but it was far from it. On accident, I let out a lite laugh out loud because she was singing her heart out but damaging ears in the process. I know, I'm going to hell, but if you laughed, you are too. As the preacher's daughter, I was expected to be in church every Sunday as a child. However, now eighteen, my interest to attend had declined. The only reason I continued to attend was to keep the peace in my household and to see Azriah.

He was Deacon Black's son, like me, he too was eighteen headed to college. Our friendship had taken on a new meaning as we grew closer but didn't claim each other. Too young to be tied down, but he was potential long-term boyfriend material. However, Mommy Dearest had a plan for me, but she was mistaken. Marriage wasn't a conversation for me regardless of hard she pushed. Besides, if I'm meant to marry it will happen in due time with the person God chose.

What seemed like hours later, church ended, and my mother returned my phone as promised. I helped Gabby stack the hymn books on the shelves and clean the communion glasses, afterward I disappeared to find Azriah for a few minutes alone. Eventually, we found each other long enough to hide and play in a closet. It was bogus of me to have sexual urges in the Lord's house. The devil used me and I didn't fight it. Close to one-thirty in the afternoon my family was able to finally lock up and head home. Four hours of church on Sundays felt like a day in summer school without air condition. Gabby sat quietly in the backseat with me as I texted my boo back and forth until the vehicle stopped. Like always, my butt was the first to hop out straight through the front door.

* * *

THE SECOND WE got home from church, I went upstairs for a five-minute shower. Oiled up with cocoa butter lotion, I slipped on a cute peach sundress that wasn't too revealing. I stood in the mirror attached to my dresser for a half hour fooling with my hair; trying to find the right style to hide my ears. They looked like elf ears, so I always tried to cover them. My mother walked into my room unannounced as she did frequently.

"Mom, I would appreciate it if you would knock and keep your nose out of my business for once! I get good grades, I'm not pregnant, and go to church as you require of me. Can I pick my boyfriend?"

"Bad enough you drove Tia away with your smothering to the point that she hardly visits now. I love you, but sometimes you're over barring actions make me want to run away or something. Can a sista get a break?" I raised my hands palms up fed up with the mother of the year.

"I tried that with your sister Tia and what happened? Do you know the story?"

"Not really, but I'm sure you are about to tell me." I loved to be sarcastic towards my mom because it got under her skin. She didn't believe in hitting, but she would curse in a second.

"I sure am, smart-ass," she said as she sat down at the foot of my bed. "A boy went to jail, and I lost a good friend at the same time. I gave her the freedom to stay the weekend with my girlfriend, Angie Barnes, who had five daughters and a son. Your fast tail sister, Tia, used the girls as a cover to mess with the boy. When she returned home from her fun-filled weekend away, life was all right. Until dinner when she didn't realize the Hickeys all over her body. Ya daddy automatically started shouting and speaking in tongue."

"What? I didn't know that," I said shocked as if I was talking to my friend from school.

"Chile, that boy sucked all on her neck, arms, breasts, and legs. I was livid, but Ecclesiastes 7:9 and Job 12:12 got me through from choking your sister. She was only in middle school, and Angie's son was a man. I had to do what was necessary as a mother and call the cops because Tia was a minor."

"Dang. The police really? How much older was he?" I sat on my bed with my left foot on the ground and my head in my hand. Tia didn't tell me she was reckless as a teenager.

"Long story short, Angie's son Kelan went to jail, and she never spoke to me again. Her daughters tried to cast Tia out of all the activities. It took a few months to smooth things other in the church. By then it was a thing of the past, yet Angie stopped attending Calvary."

"Wow, that is one heck of a story. Is that why the two of you always fight? Sometimes I wish we could have a night together just us ladies. Maybe you two can set aside your differences for the sake of bonding with your children."

"We shall see, in the meantime, pray on it. See you downstairs in ten. Don't be late"

"Okay, ma'am."

When she left, my attention turned back to my appearance in the mirror one more time before joining the family. Walking down the stairs, I instructed Siri to send Tia a text about dinner. She quickly replied back, declining. In a way, it was perfect since an outsider would be at the table. I'm sure my mom didn't want Deacon Black hearing about the nightmare dinner from hell. At the bottom of the stairs, my father strutted past me to open the door. My future husband stepped inside looking like a Reese Cup. Licking my lips, I stepped down alongside of him.

"Connie, our dinner guest has arrived," my dad announced when we walked into the dining room.

Everyone sat down to join hands for prayer. How awkward was it to be seated next him knowing we had foreplay action in the closet at church? My dad kept prayer short and sweet. The sight of perfectly golden brown baked chicken, potatoes, and corn on the cobb were mouthwatering. The first to pass his plate, my dad requested two thighs, Gabby two drumsticks.

"What pieces do you prefer son?"

"I like the thighs too Sir," he said in a sarcastic manner that made me giggle. As a family, we enjoyed the food and each other's company without incident. It helped that he was Deacon Black's son, a stand-up young man with goals. That is why I loved him.

Dinner went better than expected only because my sister wasn't at the table. Sad to say, it was the God's honest truth. It shocked the heck out of me that my mama didn't give him hell. Afterwards, I walked him out to his car for a moment alone. As much as I wanted him to stay over, I had more planning to do before we crossed that line. He was the one I wanted to take my virginity. A mutual decision between us let me know sex wasn't his main motive to be with me. "You survived dinner with the Wallace family, congratulations. It was nice, we enjoyed your company. When you coming back?"

"Anytime you invite me. Aye, my parents are out of town for at least a week if you want to sneak over. We could Netflix and Chill or do what you want to do."

"Ooh yes, we could have total privacy. Count me in baby. Man." With both hands, I grabbed his head and planted a kiss on his lips."

"Damnnnn, look what you just did," he took my hand and placed it on his manhood. Ah, it was hard, long, and curved to the left. For a young man, his piece was a nice size.

"Wow. This is what I have to look forward to? Damn, I can't wait to get it."

"Goodnight Lauren, I really have to go now. My thang is hurting and you turning me on, it's making me crazy. See you tomorrow I hope." He kissed me on the forehead then got inside his Mazda and pulled off.

* * *

UNABLE TO SLEEP, I picked up my iPhone from the stand to text Gabby. Sometimes she would draw through the wee hours. The grey bubble let me know she was awake when she walked into my room with a big bag of Smartfood White Cheddar popcorn and a bottle of Aquafina. "Hey, Sis." Gabby plopped down in the beanbag chair, making herself at home. Her curly jet-black hair was platted into four flat twists with a scarf to cover the forehead and edges.

"What's keeping you from getting a night's sleep?"

"Azriah. I think I'm in love with him; he makes me feel so many things at once. His voice, smell, touch and everything about him, drives me crazy."

"I noticed yall at dinner all giddy and flirty. It's cute and follow your heart. Both of you are only eighteen, but sometimes feelings don't lie. Take it slow and remain true to each other," Gabby suggested as she took another handful of popcorn to her mouth.

"That's the problem--I'm scared that when we go off to college things will change. Our plans now will certainly change from now until the moment we move but at this point. I don't want to be with another guy."

"Well, as long as you both communicate and trust in God to help, live life sis and stop worrying. You gotta live while you can. That means making mistakes, multiple boyfriends, or whatever. Just live right."

"Word up. Thanks. I love you, chica. Hey, why aren't you asleep? Yo ass up snacking," I questioned as she giggled.

"Just not sleepy. I was in bed watching Mary Mary until sleep came my way. It never came so I grabbed popcorn and a Snickers candy bar. I'm going back to my room to resume my show! Love you, sis, night."

"You funny. I'm going to lay here and read a book on Kindle. Love you too." She closed the door behind her. That was a good thing about having sisters, a constant friend. She would listen to me babble only adding her two cents when needed. These were times I really missed my big sister living in the house too. She let me tell her any and everything with judging plus she had crazy stories from back in the day. I tried not to corrupt Gabby with my venting, but it didn't seem to bother her.

I turned over with my phone in hand. I opened the Amazon Kindle app to resume my spot in The Other Side of the Pastor's Bed by Kayla Andre. The more I read, it became clear that church folks, including pastors, can fudge up. My dad was a good man, but this made me wonder about the skeletons in his closet. With intentions to only read a little more, I finished the book and started part two. By four in the morning, sleep finally crept up taking me under.

Five hours later the alarm buzzed, but I quickly hit the button to stop it. It was my day off from Best Buy and all I wanted to do was be lazy. I yawned, rubbed my eyes, and got up to relieve myself. Without any socks on my bare feet, the cold tile floor made me move fast. I washed my hands and flew back to my warm bed. A habit of mine was to browse Facebook when I woke in the mornings. It was to be nosey, watch funny videos, and post funny memes. Hunger pains alerted me it was breakfast time, but I know my mom had already cooked and cleaned up the kitchen.

I put my phone on the charger and made my way down to the kitchen area to make strawberry and cream oatmeal. Two packs usually did the trick for me. I filled the tea kettle with water and placed it on the front right eye. While the water slowly warmed, I got a bowl and the packets of oatmeal from the cabinet. Just when it seemed my parents had left, my dad walked in with his phone to his ear. On his way past he leaned in and kissed me on the cheek, he vanished into the basement. I poured each packet in the bowl as the high pitch whistle of the kettle sounded. I poured the boiling hot water into the bowl making sure not to add too much.

Hot cereal was my favorite because it filled me up for a few hours. My oatmeal had to be perfect, not too thick or soupy. I stirred it as the steam streamed towards my face. With a quick prayer, I dug into the warm delicious goodness until the bowl was emptied. With a small cup of orange juice, my hunger pains ceased. I washed my dishes and returned to my room for more R&R: relaxing and reading. Before getting in bed, I went to the bathroom to wash my face, brush my teeth, and then grabbed the IPad mini. It was so many books to read on my Kindle that I planned to get through. Back under the covers, my head was propped on the pillow.

The next series was titled *The Other Side of the Pastor's Bed* by Kayla Andre. After I finished part one, my thoughts about my daddy resurfaced. I wondered what type of stuff he was hiding, but then let it go because my dad was too perfect for drama. By dinner time I finished part two and three; that whole series was a five-star read.

The faint knock on the door directed my attention to the clock as I tossed the heated iPad on the bed. The more books I read by dope authors, the more I wanted to write something of my own. By the time I got out of the bed and opened the door, no one was there. The whiff of sloppy joes and corn roused my taste buds.

"Nice of you to join us, Missy. The food is still hot." My mother said with sarcasm in her voice. I didn't pay her any mind but apologized anyway as I sat next to Gabby.

"Sorry, I was reading and lost track of time. This day off is what I needed."

"We all need a day off, Baby Girl. Enjoy it now because when you enter your career phase; off days will come sparingly."

"Tell her, Baby," my mom added her two cents like always.

With two nice sized sloppy joe sandwiches, corn, and plain potato chips, I felt a nap in the making. Food and reading were my two favorite things to do in my spare time aside from spending time with my boyfriend. While at the table, there was more chewing than talking which made me happy. It seemed like the only time I could really enjoy the food was when my mother didn't have a reason to chastise. It was very seldom that it was so quiet during meal time. It made me wonder if my parents were up to something. If they were hiding something, I couldn't notice it.

CHAPTER 8

Gabrielle Wallace

I'm a sixteen-year-old girl who did everything right, obeyed my parents, and didn't cause trouble. Unlike my two sisters, I loved the church life because I didn't have to try to fit in with the other teens my age. Around the church my whole life, my parents made sure I kept busy with children choir, Bible study, and Sunday school. You name it, I participated. I was the only child who obeyed. I was my mom's favorite child, which was somewhat wrong. Nevertheless, life wasn't so bad being the pastor's kid because they taught me how to love, forgive, be compassionate, and most importantly, to be thankful. I've met some of the young people who attended church. They experienced rough home lives or dealt with the daily struggles of living right.

Like any teenager, I watched certain movies with profanity, but tried to steer clear of too much of it. I also liked to get my nails done, experiment with hairstyles, and watch what my big sisters did. From time to time Tia would host a slumber party with pizza, wings, and movies with Lauren and me. They kept me doing girly stuff, therefore I never displayed the average dike or stud look. I was average height, with honey-colored skin. I had full lips and slanted eyes. They were my best features; at least that's what people say. My long, natural, curly hair sat on my shoulders. When straighten, it touched the middle of my back. The shrinkage was real but natural hair was the best.

Sheltered from the crazy world; I kept myself busy by helping my mom in the kitchen, put together jigsaw puzzles and sketched random images that caught my eye. With not many friends, I was known as a square by classmates once they realized peer pressure didn't break me. Was it a crime to want clean working lungs and a functional liver? Polluting my body wasn't something that appeased me so instead of following the "cool kids" the church was my hang out spot.

A student at Calvary Christian High School, the education was excellent. Most teachers cared, and the parents donated thousands of dollars to ensure their kids well-being. My school consisted mostly of smart and snobby students whose parents were clergy, lawyers, doctors, or major business folks. Both Tia and Lauren attended this same high school; it was no wonder their behavior changed. A majority of the students got high and slipped to have sex in the bathroom whenever possible. Me, I just minded my business and kept out of trouble. The biggest issue of mine was keeping my crush on Brianna to a minimum. Yes, I'm an in the closet lesbian. That girl was drop dead gorgeous, the type to have all the guys bow to her feet.

Brianna was about five-three, slim with a nice backside, and her skin was like a smooth creamy caramel. Two of her best features were her smile and personality. We had two classes together every day and our desks were side by side. She had no idea how hard it was daily to sit next to her as just a friend. People had the notion that most church kids were sneaky or disobedient. Not me, I was obedient, well mannered, and polite. No one ever suspected me of anything, nor did they know I was a lesbian. I hid my secret well, but it wasn't easy seeing a person every day knowing a line could never be crossed between us.

Each day I prayed for the feelings and thoughts I had about Brianna to stop, but they continued. My father always preached about how God never made mistakes, nor did he give us more than we could bear. Well, I wish I could ask him about my situation because the burden of hiding it overwhelmed me at times. One night I had a dream that made me scared to go back to sleep. The act of sin was something I hadn't committed but I assumed the dreams were just as bad. My sisters always teased me about how much time I spent at church without complaint. In actuality, it was my way to repent for the dirty thoughts that would shock anyone who knew me.

In a household like mine, my sexual identity wasn't something I could just open up about to my parents. A few times I almost mustered up the confidence to reveal my truth, but chickened out. My belief that being open and free about who you are wasn't something my mother would understand. Set in her ways, she had those old school beliefs that God made man and woman--nothing other than that. Despite her views on LGBT related topics, she was still the woman who birthed me. Her high regard for me to be a saint smothered the person I really was. School served as an escape from being the perfect daughter and person my family thought I was. It is also where I learned how to play the role, observe and listen without showing my hand. Our school was more like a mini college because we could leave for lunch, go to a quiet location to study or sleep, and get away with breaking the rules. I went to all my classes and watched the company I kept. Only thing interested me was serving God, Brianna, and getting good grades.

CHAPTER 9

Tia Wallace

A five-forty alarm woke me the next morning. It was a school day, so I needed to be on time. Without disturbing my friend's sleep, I slipped out of her house without a peep. By eight-thirty I had freshened up, was dressed and at my kitchen table eating breakfast. Breakfast was something I tried not to skip because otherwise, it was hard to concentrate with a growling stomach. The apple cinnamon oatmeal filled my tummy with a full sensation that lasted through until noontime. Before I became an exotic dancer, my life was boring as a professor, yet I didn't complain. With two younger sisters and a best friend, they made my days enjoyable. As a professor, I worked at a college that was predominantly white, yet I loved the environment. Only a few faculty and staff of color, I didn't socialize much at the campus events. It bothered me to be around individuals who smiled in your face as if they're for change and diversity. Half of them white folks cut funding for programs geared towards multicultural students' engagement. People would be surprised at the politics that happened at UW institutions. Nonetheless, I loved working with the students; that was my main reason for dedicating my time.

Milwaukee College of Wisconsin

With fifteen minutes to spare, I sat in my car listening to Shady 45 on Sirius Satellite Radio. They were going in on the whole Kanye West and Kim Kardashian mess--pure entertainment. I enjoyed coffee and other people's drama before my day got started. When I exited my vehicle, I glanced to my left to notice some construction workers. Not thinking anything of it I proceeded to gather my purse, work bag, and coffee mug. As I strutted towards the office building something told me to glance at the men. That's when I caught the white and black guy looking at me. I flashed a smile and kept walking. Wearing a blue and white tie-dye sundress must have been the reason for their stare. My booty had an extra jiggle with each strut. Sundresses were the best thing invented.

"Ms. Wallace, may I ask a question before you collect our response papers?"

"Yes. Ask away Richard," I replied as I handed papers back to his classmates.

"Why do we have to write these papers? I mean understand but are they necessary?"

"Everything you do in my class is necessary to help shape and mold you into long-life scholars. Attending events on campus and then writing about your experience is not just to keep me busy grading, but to help you become aware of the things going on around the world."

"Thanks for answering. I understand the purpose, but sometimes I get tired of writing papers. I'll shut up now."

"Please do."

"Robert cut it out," I said as I playfully popped him with his paper. Robert was a smart kid. He just liked to be the class clown, but it wasn't going that way in my class. I handed all papers back then went to the front of the class. The moment I turned my back to write on the whiteboard, the chatter started. With fifteen minutes left of class, I had to get their attention for five. Facing them, I cleared my throat and all eyes were on me.

"I want each of you to write these three goals on the board in your planner. Highlight and underline them. The next time we meet, each of you will tell me your plan to accomplish each goal. We all on the same page?" Everyone shook their heads as if they understood my request. "Okay, you are dismissed! Have a good rest of your day."

"Bye Ms. Wallace," each of the said as they walked out of the classroom.

After class, I sat for a few minutes to unwind in peace as I checked my phone for missed calls and messages. To give myself free time at night, it was a habit of mine to print and alphabetize assignments while at school. It was a way not to take work home with me. Immediately, I grew frustrated because my students were so damn hard headed. I repeated myself all the time and they still didn't listen. Repeatedly I have told them when our online drop box doesn't work, to forward assignments to the class email or even my personal email to ensure I got it. Huh, those students found every excuse in the book not to get their work in on time. I entered a big fat zero for those students and then gathered my items to head out.

Landing Strip Lounge

It was a decent one for me because my special friend spent every last dime he had. Deon was tall with fair skin as if he was mixed with creole. Toned and chiseled with the perfect body, he looked edible with money. His cognac-brown eyes were so damn attractive; I found myself staring at him. This brotha gave me orgasms twice a week just on looks alone. The downside was when he had two or more drinks, he started boring me with his mama attachment problems. That blew my buzz real fast too, but I twirled my ass on him and danced while he vented and stuffed one hundred dollar bills in my shorts. Once the song was over, I gladly eased out of his lap and stood to my feet.

"Coco, I hope to see you next week," Deon said hesitant to let go of my hand.

"Same place, time, and price baby," I said while he let go of his grip of me. When I walked away from him, he had empty pockets and a situation inside his pants. With my three thousand tucked everywhere; I paid my house fee, the DJ, and the house mother. Back in the changing room, it was butt and breasts from wall to wall. I was dying to get up out of that place. In the process of getting dressed, I could hear this chick bragging about her customer being a baller. It was hard to take her little ugly, black ass seriously. I saw the guy she was talking about. That nigga was just as ugly as she was, but I guess there is somebody for everybody.

"You quiet tonight, Coco," Nakia uttered over the chatter in the background.

"My bad girl, I got a killer headache and I still have papers to grade," I responded as I buttoned up my shirt. Her locker was two down from mine as we faced each other.

"You have a decent night?"

"Not too bad. What about you?" I inquired.

"I got about three stacks or so. Girl, these poor men tell me their life story while drowning their sorrows in a bottle. I won't complain because it's paying my bills."

"I feel you, Nay Nay. I have one too and the crazy thing is he appears to have a perfect life. Oh well, I got my issues to deal with."

"Tell me about it," Nay Nay said as she closed her locker.

She put her coat on and I was two steps behind her as I locked my locker, zipped my coat and grabbed my bag. With my money hidden in my bag, I walked out the door with Nadia. We always parked next to each other when we worked on the same nights. With our pepper spray and keys in hand, we approached our vehicles simultaneously as we got inside. I pulled off behind her for two blocks before turning off at the streetlights on Newcomb Street. I made it home before two in the morning. The first person I called was Queen. We grew up together, but once high school came around and puberty hit, I was sent to Calvary Christian High School while she attended public school.

She was the only person in my inner circle who knew about my extra-curricular activity. As I waited for her ugly butt to answer the phone, I reach under my mattress with my left hand in search for my stash of Blueberry Kush.

"What it do, Chocolate Luv?" she said answering the phone.

Queen always called me by that name ever since middle school. "Best Friend, what are you doing?"

"In bed trying to sleep like normal people do around this time. How was your night?"

"It was cool besides Deon boring me with his mama boy ass. Girl, I swear he too fine to whine like a little girl."

"Damn, is he really that bad? Honestly, I don't know why you bother with that place. You are too good to be shaking it up and showing off your beautiful body to strangers. You need to quit that damn job."

"Here we go," I rolled my eyes not trying to hear what she was saying. My blunt was ready to be smoked. "Queen please don't lecture me; I have parents for that. I just wanted to vent for a minute with my best friend."

"Okay, I'm done but you can't blame me for caring about you."

"And I'm truly grateful that you care about my well-being and safety. I just wanted to call, vent, and let you know I made it home. I'm about clean myself up and puff on this Blueberry Kush."

"Girl yo ass about to be out the moment yo head hit the pillow! Well, hit me up when you're free, we need to do dinner or something."

"Yes, I agree, and we will link up real soon, I promise. Until then, thanks for answering your phone when I call no matter the time. I love ya girl!"

"Anytime BFF! Talk to you later."

"Night," I mumbled as the call ended then tossed the phone on the bed. I stripped out of my clothes and walked my naked self into the bathroom as my bare feet slapped against the floor. I walked inside the shower and twisted the knob as the water poured on me getting my hair wet. "Shit," I shouted as I wiped my forehead with the palm of my hand. I stepped back and grabbed my shower cap before stepping back inside. By then the warm droplets thrusted against my body, giving me the relaxed feeling. Taking a shower was one of the best feelings because the water made me forget my troubles. It was like my meditation moment each day, just me alone without interruptions. Lathered up in soap, I rinsed off good before turning off the water and wrapped in a bath towel.

To release some of the steam, I opened the door as I did a quick rub down with Pink Chiffon body lotion. I slipped on a thin night-gown on over my head and hit my armpits with some powder fresh deodorant. With a snack drawer in my bedroom within arm's reach, I slithered into bed. With my ashtray, phone, and remote on standby, I toked up watching the movie *Half Baked* with Dave Chapelle. The blueberry aroma of the marijuana had my room cloudy. Midway through the movie, I became comatose and the munchies hit me.

Sleeping late wasn't something I had the luxury of doing all the time with two jobs. It was mandatory to do morning workouts to keep my body ready for dancing at night. With a free membership, there was no excuse for me not to use it as much as possible. In decent shape to start, I had to do cardio for at least thirty minutes to an hour max. Then a little muscle building was necessary too, but I enjoyed it because exercise was important. Up by seven, I threw on some yoga spandex bottoms and top. I gathered my phone, keys, and wallet and was out the door. I hopped in my Tesla and backed out the driveway, headed to Planet Fitness.

"Tia, is that you?" A voice from behind made me turn my head slightly left, to find Nakia by the dumb bells.

"We got the same thing in mind huh. Glad to see you, we can be partners. Not to mention I get to see your secret routine."

We laughed as she showed me the machines she tended to use along with the different types of butt exercises. Afterwards, she suggested breakfast at a nearby diner she claimed served the crispiest bacon ever. Over the meal, she continued to provide me with other tips in regard to dancing. By eleven-thirty I was back home, show-ered, and in bed. I needed rest in order to get through dinner with my family later that evening.

* * *

I LIVED APPROXIMATELY an hour from my parents' house and it was worth the gas and drive. My daddy, I could deal with but my mom, she was beyond fake--dramatic. Our love-hate relationship ran deeper than most knew about. Nevertheless, she was still my mother.

Sunday dinner meant the world to my father, so I took a day off each Sunday from being petty. As the oldest, more expectations were placed upon me and the more my mother pushed me, the more, I resisted.

Huh, I wonder how long we will sit as a family tonight before the wicked witch gets on my last nerves, I thought as I parked next to Lauren's Bronze Fire Metallic Ford Fusion. I got out and looked up at the Victorian style two-story home my family resided in. On the walk up the stairs, my thoughts wondered as I questioned how financially stable my parents were to be able to afford it. I prayed my daddy wasn't a scammer or a fraud pastor because our family would be shamed.

Inside the house, it was fresh and clean as if my neat-freak mother had just dusted in the foyer and living room. To avoid seeing her, I walked up the Victorian flair curved wooden double staircase. To the left lead to my sisters Lauren and Gabby bedrooms, a balcony, and two bathrooms. To the right was my parents' bedroom, sitting room, and a balcony. Their bedroom was far enough from my sisters not to hear them. Growing up I used to sneak my friend Eli Brown into the house and we would slip and smoke joints outside on the balcony. Eli was like me, the black sheep of the family because he refused to let his father, Deacon Brown, run his life. Umm, that brotha was too fine but we were strictly friends.

Up the stairs, I knocked on Lauren's door twice as a warning before I bust through the door. "What's up little sis," I hugged her and plopped down on her purple beanbag chair. I looked her up and down as she stood in front of her body mirror.

"Big sister I have a dilemma, and you are the only one trustworthy."

She turned to face me. "Oh, this should be interesting," I said looking her dead in the face. My sister tended to be sneaky and smart when she did her little dirt.

"Spill it. What did you do or what do you plan to do?"

"Tia, I love you because you know me so well. I want to do the nasty with Azriah, but we need to make sure our plan is airtight. I follow all of Mommy Dearest rules, so I'm doing it."

"You are eighteen so technically, you can consent. Just make sure you use condoms and examine his manhood before turning out the lights. Make sure he doesn't have bumps or anything that's not normal. Who am I to stop you. Just make sure if you say stop he does, or if he says no, you stop."

"Look at you, giving me the modern-day birds and the bee's story, Ms. Hickey."

"What?" I shouted as I covered my mouth with my hand. I couldn't believe she told Lauren that story.

"Mom did not tell you about Kelen and her losing her friend story! That woman loves to bring up the past. I feel bad enough he went to jail for something I consented to. Kelen was fine and the only reason I loved to hang at the church. Wednesdays were youth group for high schoolers, and even though he was not a part of our group, he worked on the church after hours."

"I've never heard you say you like church before."

"I used to until Daddy tried to get me to go to seminary school. Anyway, I made friends with his sisters, so I could get close to him and it worked. Ms. Angie let me spend the weekend at her house and it was beyond joyful for me. To get from under this roof for two days was a dream. I was infatuated with Kelen, who was at least twenty-two at the time. He showed his interest in me too. He would lick his lips when I walk past, or I would let him feel on me quickly during Saturday Ministry."

"You're the reason mama so strict on Gabby and me. You were a little hot tamale I see. Get to the hickey part because mom was livid as she told the story."

"Did she start spitting out scriptures and fussing?"

"You know it," Lauren said as we laughed at our theatrical mother.

"Well, the first night went slow and boring until late night around nine o'clock.

He came home, and by then four of the five girls were asleep and the other on her phone. In their rooms, I slept on a pull-out bed near

Kelen's room. By eleven, it was lights out except the television. It was dark enough for him to slip in my bed unnoticed."

"I promise I had no idea it was that many hickeys on my body until morning."

"You should have seen been here to see mama's facial expressions as she told me how you let him suck all over you. Oh, she also said she wanted to choke you too."

As soon as we laughed out loud a knock at the door cut our fun short as our mom, First Lady Wallace, peeped her head in. Lauren and I looked at each other as we held in our laughter.

"Hello, Mother it's nice to see you on this blessed day!"

"My sarcastic child, I'm glad you made it for dinner this evening," she said as she turned her head towards my sister.

"Lauren, Azriah's parents have to go out of town for an unexpected visit to his in-laws. So, he will hang around with us for dinner and such, beginning tomorrow. For the next few days. Please behave yourself, and you are not to be alone with that boy! See you both downstairs in the next three minutes."

When my mom made the statement, she looked back at me longer than I cared for. She walked out the room, closing the door behind her. Once the door completely closed, Lauren started dancing because her dilemma was solved. Daddy had to be at the church almost every day all day, and with the many boards and committees my mom served on, Lauren could sneak next door if she chose to. That is something I would have tried at her age.

"Let's get downstairs before we are summoned," Lauren said once she stopped dancing.

I huffed as I extended my hand for my sister's help to get up from the bean bag as we headed downstairs. On the way, we stopped in the visitor's bathroom to wash our hands. My back pocket vibrated, the vibration made me jump and orgasm at the same time. Off guard, I shouted "OOOH!" which made my sister look at me with the side eye. I pulled the phone out and used my left thumbprint to unlock it. There was a message from Queen and a missed call. Not important at the moment, I locked the phone back and returned it to my pocket.

By the time we got to the end of the staircase, our father had walked through the door. This man didn't miss dinner no matter what his agenda entailed because my mom would not let him live it down. Also, because he loved to eat and never missed a meal a day since he was born. Any other time I was ecstatic to see my father, but what happened at the club made me nervous. Hiding my emotions were hard when it came to situations like this one.

"Hey, Daddy," Lauren and I said in unison as he hugged us. I quickly broke free from his hug; still disappointed in him. His eyes shifted back to Lauren as he tried to avoid contact.

"Both of my girls laughing and having fellowship together is a beautiful thing, praise Him. Where is Gabby?"

"Probably helping in the kitchen," Lauren answered as we took our usual chair at the dining room table. The food looked scrumptious displayed on the long antique cherry wood table. Gabby appeared carrying a small dish of potato salad that only my dad and I ate. Once all butts were in a seat, we joined hands as my father said a prayer over the food. All I heard was amen then went for the potato salad, macaroni and cheese, collard greens, and fried chicken. An excellent cook; my mom prepared meals as if it was for a television show. I guess that was one her dreams before becoming the First Lady of Calvary.

"I see somebody brought an appetite this evening. Guess all that teaching and grading mentally drains you huh?" my dad asked me as I scooped a forkful of mac and cheese in my mouth. I nodded my head up and down in an effort to keep from speaking, but it didn't last long.

"So how many students do you teach, Dear," my dad asked as my mom threw me a shady look. She was always sour about my choice to be a professor instead of the wife of a reverend. My dad wanted me to go to seminary school, but I went to UW-Madison instead to earn a bachelor's degree in Psychology and a master's in Human & Family Studies.

"Daddy, I have twenty-eight students this semester which isn't that bad compared to last semester with fifty-three. College students are a trip, but I enjoy what I do."

"I'm glad baby girl, even though I wanted you to follow in my footsteps."

"C'mon now. Don't go there,please," I said shaking my head because I could feel the devil about to use my body. Whenever my dad talked about me becoming a pastor, my mother would suck in her teeth and mumble.

"Yes, Charles don't go there. Gabby has what it takes to continue the family profession of serving God's people; our beautiful, perfect child. Besides, Tia has too much baggage to even consider that option. Teaching is where she should stay."

"Umm, you are not perfect Mrs. high almighty, First Lady Wallace. I hate it when you talk as if I'm not right here. This is why I hate coming over here because this lady is impossible." It kept everything in me from blurting out the secret about my father but because it would hurt my sisters I remained quiet.

"Hey, ladies, knock it off right now! I don't understand why you two argue like this all the time. Calm down and stop it! Need I remind you of James 1, 19:20. You both are so quick to speak instead of listening."

My father tried to mediate and to keep from using profanity, he would shout out bible verses instead. Lauren and Gabby stared like nothing had just happened and continued stuffing their faces. For five minutes there was peace amongst us all as I sat quietly in an effort to bite my tongue. My eyes shifted around the table at everyone before I caught a case of diarrhea of the mouth and just lost it.

"When you say baggage, are you implying I'm the biggest sinner? I know you feel like I brought shame to our family. I'm sure you have skeletons in your closet too while you are trying to cast stones my way. All I wanted to do was show up for dinner and have a meal like a normal family. Wishful thinking," I stated and excused myself from the table. The Wallace family put on a good show when eyes were on us but behind closed doors--we were sinners. My baby sister Gabby was the only true saint of the household, a young innocent soul.

I stormed out the house as Lauren ran behind me. The breeze of fresh air revitalized me, it felt so pleasant. The devil lived in that house which is why I had to leave. Lauren approached me with her hands up in the air.

"Tia, what the heck happened in there? Why do y'all always go for each other's throat?"

"Sister, you won't understand."

"Try me," she said as she stood with her arms crossed in front of her.

"Lauren, she is so controlling and spiteful. It drives me crazy, Sis! As the eldest child, I've had the pressure on my shoulders to be perfect. You live inside of the horror house." My frustrations always seeped out via lashing out.

"Well get yourself together because I have boy troubles you have to help me with."

"Lauren, you don't need my help with Azriah. You got this. Aye, remember condoms and the words stop or no. I love you twin, be good. I'm going home to grade papers and watch ratchet television."

"Okay, thanks! Be safe and text me when you make it. Oh, wait. You said there was something serious we needed to talk about. What was it?"

"I'll tell you another time, Sis. It doesn't matter right now anyway."

We hugged then I climbed into my ride as she ran up the stairs back inside and closed the door. I started the engine, turned on my radio and buckled up then drove off. Straight home, I made it safe and texted Lauren as promised. I handled my hygiene duties and slipped on a night t-shirt to sleep in.

On Sunday nights by ten-thirty, my school bag was usually packed, and work clothes laid out. I taught mostly freshman students Mondays, Wednesdays, and Fridays at Milwaukee College of Wisconsin. I taught two-hour class sessions three times a week. Fridays were optional. Some students requested a class on Friday when big assignments were on the line.

In my giant bed with plush covers, I reach in my nightstand drawer for the ashtray and blunt I had tucked away. Queen ass called me the moment I picked up my phone to browse Facebook. On speakerphone, my hands were free to spark the blunt.

"What up, Best friend? I literally just picked up the phone as yo ugly face popped on the screen."

"Chick, you love my face. Don't even front." She joked. It was obvious she was smoking too from the sound of her cough. We were so in sync with each other to have a smoke session over the phone. I told her about the incident at dinner and we joked until our high tales passed out. Dave Chappelle, Queen, and weed was my nighttime aide until I passed out in a deep sleep.

astor Charles Wallace

While my wife was away for a few hours, I soaked in the tub for a good hour. It was very seldom I had quiet alone time to do nothing but relax. It was a way to receive peace and understanding. There had to be a solution to keep Tia and Connie from screaming at each other all the time. Those two were so much alike that they butted heads on almost everything. I loved my daughter and wife with all my heart, but it was time for an intervention. I tried my best to intervene, but it was time to seek outside help. I stood up and stepped out of the Jacuzzi tub. With a quick pat down, I used a one-hundred percent Egyptian cotton bath towel.

My thoughts drifted back to the first few years of marriage with Connie and the struggles we face daily. Her mouth was my biggest pet peeve of mine, but as we matured together she got better. It was impossible to not love her, however, her particular ways of saying things could be over the top. Very outspoken, she made her opinions known and stood stern on her beliefs. Tia is the same way, however, she aimed to hurt Connie with words. The two acted as if loving each other was a crime. As a child, Tia craved for approval from her mom, yet all she received in return was criticism.

The unhealthy relationship they shared impacted my life in the process because it was me who tried to be neutral in each argument. It was me who had to play referee without taking sides. I was tired of it and wanted to fix the problem. I was conflicted on revealing family troubles to anyone. However, it was a desperate time and outside advice was needed.

Within a matter of minutes, I dressed and dialed the number and cleared my throat as the phone rang. "Hello, thank you for calling Christian Wellness Counseling Services. How may I assist you today?" The woman's chipper voice let me know she would assist me with no issue.

"Umm, may I ask you a question, Ma'am? I have two family members who constantly argue with each other. It is unlikely to keep them in the same room for long. It's time for an intervention but neither woman will agree to counseling. What do you recommend? Anything will help me," I pleaded with a serious tone.

"You would be surprised how many people seek assistance to get rid of family squabbles. Is there any chance of convincing both parties to seek therapy?"

"Honestly, all I can do is try, but both are very strong headed women, you follow? As a pastor and someone close to the two, outside advice would work wonders. Are there any tips you can provide me with to help guide a successful session?" The woman took a deep sigh before she answered my question.

"Well these are only recommendations, but I highly encourage some form of professional assistance. The first thing would be to talk to each woman separately to find out the underlying issues the two have. Second, try to schedule a sit down during a time in the day that both women seem to be in good spirits. Third, try to meditate without doing most of the talking. Try to let each of them to partake in engaging with each other. These are just a few things to do to start the process."

"Thank you so much. What was your name again?"

"I'm Janet. I'm glad I could assist you, Sir."

"You have a blessed day Janet! May the Lord bless you." I disconnected the call and sat in silence until it dawned on me to do a little research. I went to retrieve my iPad mini to google activities that could bring Connie and Tia's relationship closer.

"Hi, Husband. What have you been up to while I've been gone?"

"Something I don't get to do often: relax and sit still. How was your yoga session?"

"Juanita and I had a successful session and I'm in a calm mental state right now. My mind is clear, and my alignment feels great."

"That is wonderful news! You should call Tia to go with you next time. It might be good for you two to bond. I was just doing some research on activities that help strengthen mother and daughters."

"Is that so? What else have you been doing husband dear?"

"Well I prayed, did a little research and then made a call to seek advice. I needed to hear from someone not within our circle for a situation that needs fixing."

"Advice about what?"

Cautious on how to reply, I brought up the topic of therapy which wasn't the smartest thing. The idea was only a suggestion, but she took offense like only she would. Stubborn as the days are long, Connie gave me the silent treatment once I revealed the idea of counseling. I tried to be honest and open about my feelings and concern. The minute I suggested she seek outside help, she verbally ripped my head off. These were the times in marriage that drove me crazy. A divine intervention wasn't the end of the world, yet Connie overreacted.

"Why you call a stranger? I was taught to keep problems in the house. Did you forget who we are and how fast word travels?"

"Connie calm down, it's not like I called the place and told the woman detail for detail. I didn't mention names or specifics. All I did was seek assistance as a gesture to repair what has been broken."

"Charles don't get me wrong, I appreciate your persistence, but you can't make two people do something. I'll admit I'm set in my ways, however, that is who I am and that goes for Tia. You know that child is stubborn. She might've turned out differently had she not hung out with that friend of hers, Queenetta."

"You really want to blame her best friend? Let's be serious Connie, you are part of the problem. And please don't take that the wrong way. I'm just saying you don't make things easy sometimes." When her head cocked a little to the right and she placed her hands on her hips, I knew what was next."

"Charles, I just had the most relaxing yoga session to rid the negative energy. This conversation is over. Just leave it be okay?" Without another word, I let her walk away to avoid a shouting match. I went downstairs to my office to pack my suitcase, when my cell rang.

"Hello. Pastor Wallace speaking."

"Hi, pastor this is Angela. I'm sorry to call you but there is a leak in the men's restroom on the lower level. We need you to get here.

"I'm on my way. Can you inform the other pastors I'll be behind schedule?

"I will contact them the moment this call ends."

"Thank you. Please gather the information for a plumber and make sure it's not the one Deacon Black hired." When I ended the call, I was so distracted I left the house without a word to Connie. I prayed it wouldn't cause an argument later especially since it was an honest mistake. It didn't take me long to get to the church. I expected to find a huge mess but by the time I got there, the situation had been taken care of by some of the members around during the time. The plumber left his bill for me and went about his day. Phone meetings kept me occupied most of the day. I almost forgot to eat until Angela knocked on my door with sandwiches.

"Pastor, you should really take a break and enjoy this sub. All of that talking must have built up an appetite." She laid the Subway bag on my desk and sat the lemonade drink next to it. "I ordered you a ham and turkey with lettuce, cucumbers, and lots of mayo and honey mustard."

"Wow, you are so thoughtful. Thank you for this meal. I'm might not make it home for dinner, so this will hold me over until tonight. Will you be joining me?"

"I thought you'd never ask. I'll be right back."

I observed her as she retrieved her food and sat across from me.

The entire time we laughed and enjoyed each other's company, sin clouded my mind. An innocent meal together made me feel so dirty because I imagined my manhood in her mouth instead of the six-inch sandwich. A man--Godly man--was a man no less. My thoughts made me as dirty as the actual sin.

"So, where do you see yourself in the next three years? Do you aspire to do anything that was put on hold?"

"I honestly don't know the answer to that question. My goals were thrown off when hard times hit. As a little girl, I always wanted to own a nail shop; of course my dream changed again and again."

"Well it's never too late to make a dream come true. Maybe I'm the person who was to motivate you to act on your dream. Anything is possible in this day in age."

"Nice way of put things into perspective. On a serious note, I've taken interest in decorative designer and hospitality. The idea of seeing my work in magazines and even celebrity clients would be to die for."

"Today is the day you embark on a new journey of fulfilling a dream. Feel free to take off early if you would like to get started." So comfortable at my desk, I almost forgot where we were at. I wrapped up my garbage and tossed it in the trash can. A quick glance at the clock on the wall alerted me it was time to leave.

"Thank you pastor; I just might do that."

"Please call me Charles when it's us alone. It makes things less formal and serious. Now if you'll excuse me. I'd better gather my thing and get going. Pastor Jennings hates it when people arrive late."

* * *

A FEW WEEKS LATER, things heated up between Angela and me causing me to do things I'd never thought of as a married man. I'd begin to lie and stay out later than I should've all because her sex had me hooked. It had gotten to the point all I could do was think about Angela and the sin we committed.

CHAPTER 11

Queenetta "Queen" Jones

BFF's with Tia from middle school until adulthood, we talked every day. Our friendship comprised of three rules. For that reason, that we vowed to have each other's back. Rule number one was that neither of us could be afraid to tell each other the truth. Regardless of how we felt, we made a pinky swear that honesty was everything. Rule two required that we make time for each other at least twice a week for lunch, dinner, shopping, or some type of activity. She was the yin to my yang, so we talked every day. Lastly, rule number three reminded us that nothing or no one could come between our friendship. We never had to worry about breaking the three rules because she had a habit of popping up at my place to smoke with her stoner ass.

Tia was a very attractive female with an amazing cocoa brown skin and perfect body. Our friendship was a little unusual. Some frowned upon it because Tia and I had been intimate a few times. The first time we crossed the line was during a night of drinking and dancing with Reese, a mutual childhood friend. Fueled by vodka, my lust for her grew as I watched her on the dance floor. I've always wanted to have my way with her one time and that night was my venture moment.

Back at my place, we passed out in my bed. Close to three in the morning Reese, and I woke up simultaneously. Tia was out and had stripped down to her panties and a thin strap tank top. Horny, Reese freaky ass encouraged me to take advantage, and I did. The position she laid in made it easy for Reese to taste her lady parts and I took the top. I pulled each breast out and sucked the night away until she woke up in a confused state. Reese sucked on her clit and that helped relax her. Tia relaxed so much she didn't react to the seven-inch rod Reese eased inside her.

As a bisexual woman, the pleasure doubled when Tia and Reese agreed to play time. Sometimes I got wetter watching others in action, which I found odd. Moans and groans were the only sounds that came from my room that night. To this day, I got wet anytime the thought comes to mind. I let Reese hit me too. Reese was five-foot-nine with a body created by a goddess; a luring smile and a tongue that operated at any speed. Reese resembled the character Ralph Angel from the television show *Queen Sugar*.

A dark chocolate sexy ass man. I let him lick me up a few times back in the day, but the last time we hooked up was that night. Tia, Reese, and I had an understanding of what we did together. Aware of the consequences, we used protection at all times--oral included.

The next morning, the sun rays shined brightly through the blinds waking me up. Wide-awake, my eyes adjusted to the light as I glanced at Reese and Tia spooned up together knocked out. A smile flashed across my face while I quietly got out of the bed and stepped into the bathroom. The minute I finished and exited, Reese and Tia were lying in bed awake with their phone in hand.

"Morning Sleepy Heads. I hope y'all slept well. I sure did."

"Dude, I'm still high and hungry as hell," Reese stated while he scratched his head. Dressed in nothing but his red boxer briefs he strolled to the bathroom, leaving Tia and me alone. When the door closed, our chatter began like schoolchildren.

"Queen, what the heck happened? My nipples sore. Not to mention, my vajayjay hurt."

"Let's just say you should blame it on the alcohol and weed." I expressed with a little laugh just as Reese appeared.

"Why y'all get all quiet? Aye, last night was off the chain. Tia, you a little freak girl," he announced.

Tia blushed and tried to hide her face from the two of us. I could sense she was a bit uncomfortable, to say the least. This was her first time doing something so wild in the bedroom. Tia continued to lay in bed as Reese slipped his shirt on over his head. The sounds of rumbling in my stomach made it clear food was of importance.

"You staying for breakfast Reese?"

"Naw, I need to go hit the shower and then meet up with an old friend to talk business. Good looking though."

"Suit yourself. Thanks for the exceptional night. Talk to y'all soon," I blew him a kiss. Tia moved slowly around the kitchen in search of coffee. Once Reese left, I prepared sausage, hash browns, and cheese eggs for Tia and myself. Breakfast and laughs are how we started our Friday. Tia left my house close to noon to tend to her affairs. As soon as my high wore off, I showered. In the process of washing up, a quick flashback made me reminisce about Tia and Reese in bed.

* * *

MOSTLY INTO WOMEN, it was weird that Reese was the only male I was willing to sex up. A bad experience five years ago, when I was young and dumb, has haunted me; causing me to have trust issues with men. Michael was his name and he claimed to love me, would never hurt me, nor cheat. This fool did all of that and more. Liquor was both our enemies since it fueled anger and physical abuse. Without a male role model, it wasn't apparent to me that physical abuse was wrong. I hid everything from my granny for as long as possible until she spotted an unexplainable bruise on my lower back. That was the first time I ever saw that woman snap and forget her religion. I grew a backbone to stick up for myself. Without hesitation, she bussed in my apartment to teach Michael a lesson about raising a hand to me. Let's just say, she was very handy with a blade.

The way her hand gripped the switchblade amazed me, as she remained steady with it pressed against his Adam's apple. The slightest swallow or movement, she would've drawn blood. Not once did I try to stop her. It was too much fun to watch him squirm for a change. From the south, my grandmother grew up with all brothers who taught her how to be rough. Back in the day, she was a bully-- only to boys who picked on the girls. From that day, I never let a man raise his voice, hand, or anything else at me. By age twenty-two, my connection with women grew to the point that it was time to test the waters. Being with a woman was so different but it felt fitting for me and my personality. Tia was the first person I talked to about my decision to switch teams, never did she judge or discourage me.

Open about my sexual preference, life was good. Free with no one to report to or beat my ass. Single life best suited my persona. The previous relationship taught me more about myself than others: to use my head, never show emotion, and stand my ground no matter. Ever since I did, peace has done me well mentally and emotionally. With a minor setback though, a car accident was what truly gave me a new attitude. I even attended worship at Calvary twice a month. It made my grandmother happy to see a change in me.

* * *

RAIN, sun, and sounds of thunder were no excuse for me not to get my ass out of bed. Mondays were therapy days from the car accident I had several months ago. The left leg got banged up bad along with a janky neck. That was the scariest experience, but I'm thankful my life was spared. Tia always complained about her family, but they visited me several times. Even her mom paid me a solo visit. My perception of her changed a little when she finally opened up on why she didn't want Tia and me to hang. Apparently, she assumed I would turn Tia into a lesbian or something because of our closeness. I laughed out loud thinking about it. She wasn't my favorite person, but I sometimes wished she was my mother too.

Dressed in a black sundress and jean jacket, my hair was freshly cut into a short bob style. It was only therapy, but a sista had to look good at all times. I left home headed to therapy. It took up no more than an hour of my day. I wasn't tripping either because my insurance paid for it. When I arrived, the first thing I did was check in with Sarah, the receptionist. She was such a nice lady, but her voice killed my eardrums. That high pitch squeak was only tolerable for short periods.

"Hi, Sarah. I'm a few minutes early." I signed in then sat down.

"Hey, Queen! You are looking good girl. Ooh, your hair is sooo cute!"

"Thank you. It's time to change it up maybe add some color," I disclosed. Before my eyes could read the magazine in hand, Dr. Pero called for me. I placed the magazine on the table, followed behind him to the room where the heat lamp and massage chair. Therapy was like a spa day paid for by insurance.

You see I'm a product of a gambler, drug addict, and professional thieves. No mother or father in my life from birth, my granny was all I had. Her selflessness to raise me was the best thing in life. For those reasons, I avoided foster care and other horrible abuse that kids went through when bounced around the system. Fortunate enough, she and my best friend helped me stay out of mischief all the way through to recovery.

To keep the bills paid I worked two jobs in the downtown area. Obne as a Dish Inventory Specialist five days a week. The second job was more social, bartending at the Hyatt Regency. Being professional during the week and a social butterfly during the weekends kept my life interesting. My job duties at Dish included daily inventory of equipment, management of warehouse merchandise, and computer-based Excel Office tasks. It was my responsibility to manage the flow of materials and equipment.

Our team worked well together and has yet to screw up anything. My direct supervisor was very flexible on hours and compensated for overtime. On the weekends, the bartender gig was a way to unwind from the week's troubles and let loose for fun. The services I provided at the Hyatt kept me in the loop about the latest business, fashion, and entertainment. Customers talked about any and everything once the liquor took effect. With many talents and skills, bartending became a favorite hobby to pass time when I broke up with Michael. A few odd jobs at a time helped me learn how to mix the hell out of some drinks.

Working at the Hyatt was a piece of cake not to mention the pay wasn't bad. Plus, I've heard and seen all types of funny mess. Last weekend a couple walked up to the bar from the lobby. The guy had to be six feet tall, walnut brown skin, and super confident. Dressed in a navy blue suit jacket and slacks, he unbuttoned the jacket and took a seat. The woman complimented his attire with a black off the shoulder dress with a black sheer cover-up. Both were black, so I knew after a few drinks they would entertain me.

With a white rag, I wiped down the counters at the other end of the bar. By the time I made it back in their vicinity I heard him say, "So after this nightcap, you gonna give me some of that pudding? A nigga deserves a taste or something." My eyes widen in bewilderment as did the woman. Niggas always wanted to have sex like it was mandatory. In a professional state of mind, my mouth stayed shut, but I sure wanted to add my two cents. To hear better while being less suspicious, I got closer and asked if they needed more drinks. The guy quickly shooed me away with his attention towards the woman. She looked as if she was contemplating on fulfilling his request. Seconds later, they got up from their seats and left.

For the next three hours, I smiled, served, fixed drinks, and eavesdropped on conversations. In between bored moments, I fooled around with Snapchat filters and played iGames with Reese. By the time ten-thirty hit almost everything was stocked and ready for the changeover person. My workstation was the same way I found it, clean and ready for operation. Brian walked in with his uniform crisp and a new piercing. "Oh, I see you all fresh and clean. Everything is set for you. Have a good night," I didn't waste time clocking out. In his flamboyant voice he said, "Thanks, girl. See you next weekend," he proclaimed with an air kiss. Tickled pink with him, I waved my hand and headed out.

CHAPTER 12

ia Wallace
 Weeknights at the club were either right or slow. Strangely, I had a request from a female customer. I was nervous because I'd never danced for a woman before, but money was money. I always wanted to know what females got out of being in the club, so I used the opportunity to find out.

"May I ask why you requested me out of all these women in here umm-?"

"Stacey! Honestly, you looked approachable; you have an excellent shape, and to satisfy my curiosity. I know you can't mix business with pleasure, but I have another request. Can I come back every once in a while, for a dance or two?"

"If that's what you want. Are you in the closet or just exploring?"

"Actually, both I think. I love men from their smell to the feel of their rod, but I find myself attracted to confident women. For example, I got wet when I saw you. Your breasts are perfect to look at, but I bet they're better to suck on. I'm sorry that was out of line."

"It sure was, but thanks for the compliment. I hate to break the bad news to you, but I have issues too," I said as I took the last two gulps of Hennessy. My inner sex craving was trying to come out.

"Aye, let's move over there where it's a little darker and intimate," I said and took Stacey's hand. We relocated towards the corner where it would be hard to see us even with the cameras watching.

"This is better don't you think? Tell me more about your conflict."

"As I stated before, my weakness are beautiful breasts with perfect nipples. That is the only part of the female body I like. It's weird but that's how I feel."

Against my better judgment while giving her a lap dance, I slid her hands up to my breast. She had a tight grip. I felt her fingertips massage my nipples until they were hard as rocks. My inner gay girl came out that night and afterward I changed, packed up, and drove home. Once I showered and ate I laid my butt down and toked up while watching movies. Drifting off to sleep with my head nodding, the phone rang made me jump. My face frowned when I saw who was calling.

"Hey Daddy," I said plainly without any enthusiasm in my voice. I held the phone to my ear as he created small talk with the basic how you been and what's new type of ish. Not really up for conversation, my answers were short and sweet making me recall the night he discovered my secret. "I've been well and nothing really beside teaching and dancing."

"Honey, can I be frank? Have you thought about quitting that job? It's just I don't want to see anything happen to you. I know you keep yourself safe but there are crazy men out there that prey on young women like you."

"Daddy, is this call to chastise me or what? Otherwise I--," he stopped me from finishing my sentence.

"Tia, I'm your father and I will always be concerned about your safety. I called to apologize and set up a dinner date. We need to make amends and repair our relationship, what do you think about that?"

There was a brief moment of silence before I swallowed my pride and spoke. "Things will definitely be different for a while but yes, I'm willing to work on it. How are things at the big house?"

"Umm, your mother is mad at me for seeking options such as

counseling, your sisters are doing well, and Calvary is keeping me busy."

"So. nothing has changed then. Go figure. I don't know why she always overreacting. Seeking to counsel would help her let go of whatever anger was weighing on her. I love her but refuse to be around her if all she does is bash me."

"I know baby girl but like Ephesians 4:32 says, *Forgive one another as God for Christ's sake hath forgiven you.* Remember I've been married to her for over twenty years and it wasn't easy in the beginning."

"I'm trying but she has to be willing as well. Otherwise, it's a waste of time. Time and energy are two things she will not take. I have enough students who do that."

"Have faith, Dear. Anyway, I called to see where you wanted to meet for dinner.

Your mother and I are traveling to Atlanta, but I wanted to set something up with you now. I'm willing to meet anytime."

"Dad, regardless of my stubbornness I try to be a good daughter, however, I'm not perfect. Obviously, you and mom aren't either so I'm willing to meet with you. Just let me know when y'all get back and where you want to meet, and I'll be there."

"Thank you, Baby Girl. I'll let you go now. I need to finish packing. Pray your mother doesn't try to pack up her entire wardrobe."

A laugh escaped my mouth as I chuckled because my mother packed too much each time they travel.

"Love you honey."

"Safe travels. Love you too daddy." The call ended just as Connie joined me in the double walk in closet.

CHAPTER 13

*P*astor *Charles Wallace*

  Despite our disagreements, every year in October, my wife and I traveled with Deacon Black and his wife to a different city as guests. This year we were invited to Atlanta, Georgia. I was excited to be guest pastor at Mt. Zion Church of Christ. I loved to spread the word but hated the traveling part only because it took a lot of my energy.

  "Do you think I packed too many clothes or I should be okay with what I have already?"

  "Charles, stop overthinking and zip up the bag. Sometimes you overthink things instead of just letting it flow. You will be alright, don't worry. Let Deacon Black take the lead anytime you get worked up. The Lord has your back, and so do I."

  "Where would I be without you, woman? I'm so thankful you are my wife and First Lady! Give me some sugar," I said as I pulled her close. We shared a kiss as she loosened my tie. "Oh, I see what's on your mind. Come over here and let me undress you."

  With a dose of pleasant love making, we quickly showered in effort to be on time to depart for the airport. Fifteen minutes later the anxiety had left my body and somehow got to Connie, who was hesitant to leave our girls home alone. It wasn't that she didn't trust them, it was just a mother thing she insisted. On the way from our room, I carried the luggage down as Connie knocked on Lauren and Gabby's door.

"Girls I need you front and center downstairs, now," she announced.

At the bottom, I waited for all three of them, checking my two-toned Kenneth Cole watch. It was imperative we be on time getting to the Black's home so that we could make it to Mitchell International. With a quick clearing of the throat, I tapped the face of my watch.

"Baby don't rush me we are in good timing. Okay, girls, your father and I will be gone for three to four days tops. Lauren, because you are the one left in charge, I trust things will go smoothly. No boys, alcohol, or anything your father and I wouldn't approve of. There is plenty of food for the both of you until we return. Any questions?"

"No ma'am! We should be fine until you guys return so please don't worry about us. Enjoy the time in Atlanta, besides we can call Tia if needed."

"See honey, nothing to worry about. We have responsible children."

Connie let out a sigh before she finally accepted the fact that our girls could be trusted. She gave each a tight hug and kiss on the cheek then made her way out of the door. I mimicked my wife then carried our bags to the car. "Girls, please behave so your mother isn't busy worrying the entire time away."

"Yes, daddy! We promise," both spoke at the same time as if they were twins.

* * *

WE BOARDED our plane for Atlanta after sitting around almost two hours. Deacon Black wore a sly smile on his face as if he was up to no good. At times I wondered what went on in that head of his. Seated next my wife in first-class, everyone buckled up as the flight attendant gave us permission to turn on our cell phones. There was an audio-book by Kimberla Lawson Roby I'd downloaded a day ago, it was finally my chance to listen. It was perfect timing, I needed a way to avoid hearing Deacon Black's voice.

After take-off, a petite young woman attendant came up to us with a snack and beverage cart. With my elbow I nudged Connie. With a grin she proceeded, "Hello. Would either of you like something to drink? Or a snack perhaps?"

"Yes, two glasses of water, two bags of pretzels and two packs of cookies. My wife and I eat the same thing," I joked.

"Absolutely," was her response as she handed us the items requested and moved to the next person.

Connie wrapped her red wireless in-ear Powerbeats by Dr. Dre around her ears and tapped on her Smartphone. She liked jazz music; it helped her unwind for the almost two-hour flight. I did the same with my shock yellow headphones Lauren bought for us as a Christmas gift last year. We both sat back to rest in downtime until we arrived at our destination. The soothing voice of the narrator filled my ears causing me to nod out several times until there was no more fighting sleep.

"Ladies and gentlemen, welcome Hartsfield-Jackson Atlanta International Airport. Local time is five-fifteen and the temperature is 79 degrees. For your safety and comfort, please remain seated with your seatbelt fastened until the captain turns off the fasten seatbelt sign…"

The soft-voiced woman gave us instructions to check around our seats for personal belongings. Ready to stretch my legs I wondered if Bishop Ellis would meet up or send someone. The moment it was safe to turn on my phone I did just that and automatically messages of all kinds appeared on the screen. Sure enough, there was a message from the bishop on where to meet him once we landed. He was truly a wonderful man with a kind heart. The idea of being a guest pastor at his church always made me nervous even though it was my fifth invite.

The four of us followed behind the crowd off the plane and headed to the baggage claim area. Connie watched the carousel for our bags hoping nothing was lost. "That wasn't a bad flight at all," Diane Black voiced as she stretched her arms in the air then adjusted her purse on her shoulder.

"Ah, it feels good to walk and stretch a bit," Connie added as she used her fingers to fluff her hair.

Finally, the bags came around and Deacon Black and I grabbed them after checking the tags. Afterwards, we proceeded to the car rental counter. Rental cars and lodging were taken care of by Bishop Ellis, who greeted us. His generosity and southern hospitality never ceased to amaze. He was the founder of his own church that went from a congregation of three hundred to three thousand members. He reminded me of T.D. Jakes; bald, dark with a stocky stature. Bishop was just a little better looking minus the gap in his teeth.

"Welcom,e Pastor Wallace and Deacon Black," he shook our hands then turned his attention to Connie and Diane. He planted a kiss on the top of their hands. The two women kept their polite "in the public" smile but I knew all they wanted to do was eat and shower. Traveling was always something Connie didn't care for as the First lady. Instead, she'd rather drive--the things that woman has done for me in the name of Jesus.

"It is so wonderful to see you all. Here are your keys. Two Nissan Versa vehicles await you. Also, there are two rooms reserved for you at the Grand Hyatt Atlanta located on Peachtree Road. It's in the Buckhead neighborhood. You can park in the lot adjacent to the hotel. I'm almost sure you will enjoy the view from the High Floor King Room."

As he talked, we walked right out the door as he led the way to an uncrowded area to speak details about our visit.

"Bishop, you're too kind. Thank you again for the set-up. I'm sure ready to eat. What do you recommend?" Diane couldn't have been more serious because my stomach had been cutting up too from hunger pains.

"I understand, Mrs. Black. I'm a little hungry too. How about we go eat first then you check into your rooms to rest and rejuvenate. What do you fine people have a taste for? Soul food? BBQ?"

"Soul food. Fried chicken and peach cobbler are on my taste buds," Connie answered. With a unanimous vote, Bishop informed us about good food at Mary Mac's Tea Room. In the car, my wife and I drove behind Bishop while Deacon Black and Diane followed. Connie pulled up the menu for the establishment on her Smartphone and she read out the different items we could order. Bishop Ellis hit his right signal and turned into the parking lot. The five of us enter through the door only to have the smell of fresh fried chicken hit our noses. The sweetness of sweet yams and cornbread had me head over heels.

Barely able to move we made our way to our vehicles as Bishop served as the tour guide and lead us to our hotel. He stayed long enough to make sure nothing went wrong during check-in. "Alright, saints, enjoy your stay. Explore Atlanta and call me if you need anything. Pastor Wallace, I'm looking forward to hearing that sermon Sunday morning."

When I inserted the hotel key and opened the door, my eyes couldn't believe the view. Our room was equipped with a king-sized bed, sitting area with a sofa, kitchenette, and most importantly, an extra half bath. The further Connie and I walked inside we also noticed a dining and working area. The most beautiful part was our balcony view of Stone Mountain and downtown Atlanta.

"Honey, we need to come here more often just for the view and quietness. This place must have cost a fortune to rent for three nights. I wonder if Deacon Black and Diane's room is similar."

"I'd imagine so Dear! Thank you for traveling with me. I know how much you rather road trip than fly." I tossed my travel kit on the bed as I unpacked my luggage, hanging my suit up in the closet.

"That is what a wife does right? Compromise with her spouse because we both said vows. You don't have to thank me. Besides, I'll do a little shopping with your credit card. That will be my way of accepting your compliment."

"Woman you are so quick with that tongue, it's like you practice what to say and when to say it. Either way, that is why I love you--for being yourself."

"Always and forever," she whispered and then pressed her soft lips against mine.

"What do you say we shower and call it a night? There will be plenty to do tomorrow."

"That's fine. You go ahead. I'm about to call home to check on the girls. I know Lauren is up and has that darn phone glued to her hand. It will only take me a few minutes, I promise."

"Whatever you say, Dear," I muttered with my travel kit in hand headed to the shower. See you in a few. While washing from head to toe, Connie joined. Her fingers glided across my back like mini massage brushes. Slowly I turned towards her ready to share an intimate moment. Hot and bothered, I rinsed the soap off and stepped back so Connie could quickly wash. We made love for over an hour and the only sounds were the moans and groans we exchanged. Deep breaths, sweat dripping, and a dry throat left me exhausted.

"Wow, woman. You know how to put it on me. I'm good for a few days until I let you dose me up again."

"That's what you say now," she joked as we went to the bathroom to wash up. Afterwards, we went outside. With my arms wrapped around Connie's waist, we stood out on the balcony to enjoy the peace and calmness. Our night ended wonderfully.

The next morning, we read the daily devotion, had a good workout, and breakfast. Connie and I decided to go site-see for a few hours in downtown Atlanta. Later in the day, the women hung around our suite. They took advantage of the spa while I prepared and practiced for the sermon. As a guest pastor in another state, I did a little research on Mt. Zion and the local issues they faced. For three hours I read, sipped tea, and took breaks on the balcony. Saturday continued to be relaxing as I went through the Sprinkle of Jesus app.

The daily alerts provided advice on how to change, give up burdens, and rely on God and many others. I came up with the title "Living Right" as the sermon. Too many folks lived a foul or double life only giving part of themselves to the lord. A sinner like all, I too needed to start living right for the sake of my family. As a man of the cloth, I never meant to stray or break any commandments, yet the minute Angela used her womanly charm I grew weak. Unable to resist I committed adultery--something I deeply regretted. My wife never deserved it and I prayed she would never find out.

When I finished, my adviser gave her input. Connie took a glance at my scribble scrabble. She made a few faces, tilted her head, and then smiled. Her input was important from the structure of sermons down to what suit to wear. I made the changes and practiced again until the words flowed with ease. Sermons were important, but the deliverance had to move to the people. Once Connie and I agreed the sermon was perfect we took the liberty to enjoy more of Atlanta before turning in for the night.

* * *

THE NEXT MORNING, I thanked the Lord for waking me. He gave me another day to fulfill my purpose. To stay on schedule, Connie ordered room service. I showered then she did the same. Our spacious suite made living out of a hotel a decent experience, however, I couldn't wait to get back home. Atlanta had been a nice place to visit but I missed my girls and seeing Angela. In the mirror I rehearsed one last time making sure to pronounce words correctly. At a quarter to eight, Connie and I left for Mt. Zion. Traffic on a Sunday morning was bananas. With a few minutes to spare we made it in enough time to chat with Bishop Ellis.

"Morning Pastor Wallace. Are you ready to bless us with the word today?"

"I sure am, Bishop. Thank you again for this. Just give me the cue and I'll deliver." He gave me the rundown of how the service would proceed and how I should just follow along with him and the deacons. Speaking in front of folks was always something I took pride in; whether it was three people or three hundred. Not so much nervous, I feared the congregation wouldn't like my style of preaching. Mixed in with the members, Deacon Black and his wife took a seat in the front pew with Karen.

As I slowly scanned the mixed congregation from the pulpit, my vision was blocked as Bishop Ellis who stood before me. I sat down beside an older man who introduced himself as Deacon Harris. Before we could get acquainted, Bishop Ellis called worship to order. Folks scrambled to find a seat as silence slowly filled the sanctuary. Bishop's husky voice lead us all in prayer followed by the choir's song selection. "How Excellent" has always been a favorite song of mine. The soulful melodies were like angels as the blended voices graced my ears.

"Good morning church! It feels great to be here in worship with you. Thank you, choir, for the wonderful selection. That is one of my favorite songs. Let us keep praising our heavenly Father. Amen." I heard a few folks yell amen as I paused to take a few sips of water before I continued. "Turn to your neighbor and repeat after me. I am not perfect but I'm a work in progress. My God is not done with me."

Each person repeated my words to each other showing their ability to follow instructions but most importantly to open their minds and hearts. I slid the two-page, tri-folded sermon from my suit jacket pocket and laid them on the podium. A few glances at the text, I realized there was a different message formulating in my spirit. Right on the spot, I went impromptu.

"Church, as a guest in your house, I want you to know that I'm not perfect either. I'm a work in progress just like you. I wear this collar but I'm not without sin. Being a work in progress ain't easy but it's doable. We have to put God first. Whatever he tells us to do, we should do it because he's testing us. Change is uncomfortable but necessary if you want to live a peaceful life. You see, I've learned that a lot the troubles and pain we suffer are self-inflicted. Can I get an Amen?" I took another paused to wet my throat then decided to try something to get more reactions from the congregation. I stepped from behind pulpit to interact more as I spoke into the microphone.

"We as humans fear what change may bring. The feeling of not being in control causes us to fall back into our old ways. As children of God, we cannot be fearful or scared. Each of us were made in his image; he has a bigger and better plan. We just have to have faith and believe that our God makes no mistakes. Our purpose in this world hasn't been fulfilled yet because we are still gathered here together. With that being said, my God is not done with us."

"Amen!" A woman in the front shouted.

"I know that's right, Pastor!" Bishop's wife, Karen shouted from behind me.

"We are his soldiers. If we want change, it's up to us to make it happen. The more uncomfortable we become, is a sign that God is working. I'd like to leave you with two scriptures to ponder on and maybe read before bedtime. Romans 12 will help you reflect on your love for God and reevaluate your purpose. Proverbs 4:23 encourages you not to let people or issues influence the change you set out to make. In closing, take each day step by step and work to be a better person. Thank you."

Headed back to my seat by Connie, the round of applause made me feel relieved. The unplanned sermon made me reflect on my own life and purpose. When I sat down Connie leaned in to whisper "Good job honey. You winged it really well." Bishop Ellis called us all to stand for the offering prayer which followed communion and another offering. The closing choir selection "I Know I've Been Changed" was the perfect hymn to wrap up. After service was over, Connie and I went back to the hotel for a little R&R until dinner.

* * *

Bishop and his wife, Karen, insisted we gather together at their home for a meal and fellowship before we departed back to Milwaukee. Unable to say no, Connie and I joined the two. Deacon Black and his wife went to her parents. It was almost as if they weren't even around the entire trip. Karen prepared fried catfish, spaghetti, Hawaiian dinner rolls, with White Zinfandel wine. In the company of like-minded folks, Sunday evening was like a breath of fresh air. Time flew as the four of us learned more about each other's hobbies. Bishop even encouraged me to explore other options in the ministry right before we prepared to exit the home. We said our goodbyes and parted ways. Our flight departed first thing the next morning. Deacon Black and his wife decided to stay one more day.

CHAPTER 14

*C*onnie Wallace

We came back from Atlanta like a new couple; almost as if we had another honeymoon. Charles did better balancing the church and home. He even went as far as meeting Tia for dinner. Our family was a work in progress but who really had work to do was me. I needed to find common ground, it hurt me we couldn't share memorable moments. Charles made me realize I was turning into my mother--controlling and patronizing.

Usually, I don't go to the church office with Charles on Wednesdays, but he suggested we do lunch and go to the church for a bit. I agreed because there were a few tasks I needed to complete for Women's Bible Study. Besides, I loved spending time with him even if it was in the house of the Lord. By the time we left Applebee's and made it to the church parking lot, I felt sluggish. Something told me to eat light, but no, I had to order rib tips. As we retrieved our belongings from the back seat my stomach growled.

"Wow Charles, I'm so full that I might have to take a quick nap in the office. You should've recommended I eat something different."

"Oh c'mon, Connie, don't go blaming me because you ate that pork and caught the itis. if I would've suggested a different meal, you would've ordered ribs anyway."

I remained silent for a brief second because he was correct. "Yeah you right, but still."

"You're crazy, woman, but I still love you! Come on," he said as he wrapped his arm around me. Finally, inside the building, we walked down the set of stairs to the double office Charles and I shared.

A little after two o'clock, I felt much better while the angelic sound of Yolanda Adams played in the background of my MacBook. Typing away and praising his holy name, I got up from my seat for a moment to stretch. Walking into the other room, my husband sat writing on his legal pad. He swiveled in his russet leather seat while I sat across from him.

"Are you feeling better Honey?"

"Yes. Much better, thanks. I knew better so it's my fault. How are you coming along with the sermon for Sunday?"

"I have close to five different topics, just trying to see which will fit. Politics aren't my thing, but I feel the need to address something. When I have it all written down I will pass it to you for feedback."

"Whatever you need, Pastor."

"I love seeing you this way; happy and in good spirits. Atlanta was exactly what you needed. Speaking of, did you call your daughter yet? She's willing to put her stubbornness to the side."

"Not yet, but don't worry Charles. I will call her tonight before bedtime. I told you I'm ready to do the same. Baby steps, Honey. Besides, women have a way of doing things our way."

"I pray it does because-," he said as his sentence was interrupted by a knock on the door as it opened. In walked his secretary, Angela Johnson, with a bunch of documents in a manila folder. "Pastor Wallace, here are the items you requested. Oh, I'm sorry for interrupting," she apologized then smiled from ear to ear. All I did was watch her in silence.

"It's fine, Angela. Come on in. My wife and I were just taking a break. I'll take those from you. Thanks."

Angela was nice young lady. She did a good job around the church and even taught the Sunday school children. In my seat, I surveyed her attire from head to toe, then noticed her cute black flower earrings. Angela always dressed in something cute and appropriate. This time around--I was disappointed. She had on a short, black floral-pleated vintage skirt, a long sleeve shirt and black pumps. It was my belief that women should only wear knee-length dresses, skirts, or slacks to church.

I was also disappointed that she had the nerve to semi flirt with my husband in front of me. Her eyes did all the talking as her never-ending staring made me wonder her motive. Charles tried to ignore the contact, but my intuition let me know I wasn't tripping. A woman had a certain way of doing things, Angela was on the prowl. Nevertheless, she was on my radar now. Prompting me to figure what type of game she was playing. Light skinned, fairly young and gorgeous; I could see how Charles could fall under temptation.

After she sashayed out, I went back to my office to finish the task I started. A half hour later, Charles and I headed home. During the ride, he ran his idea by me for a clothing drive and a Saturday workshop for men and boys. Charles was so passionate about giving back and helping others; he never stopped. While I was listening to him, Angela was my main focus because I be damned her young tail broke up my happy home.

"It's so many young boys without fathers. I think pairing them together would be a good thing. The boys can learn how to properly tie ties, get advice, and gain a mentor. That could be the difference in their behavior," he said as we approached our block.

"That is a wonderful idea, Pastor. Go for it. The girls and I will help prep lunch if you want."

"I plan to talk to a few of the men that I'm sure will commit. How could I turn down your cooking?" We laughed as he turned into our driveway, not opening the garage.

When we got inside, I whipped up a fast meal of fried green tomatoes, pasta, and mini shrimps with fettuccine alfredo sauce. For dessert, we had ice cream and chocolate brownies. In the midst of our family laughter, Tia's absence saddened me. After dessert, I excused myself from the table to go upstairs for a shower. After that, I dialed Tia's number hoping she didn't hang up. To my surprise, she answered on the third ring.

"Hey Mama is everything okay?"

"Yes. Why would you think something was wrong?"

"Because you don't call me on a regular."

"I just wanted to call to chat if you have time. Your father told me you both had a good dinner. Do you want to get together soon to shop and have lunch?"

"You and dad not hiding anything are you?"

"Tia, why are you so skeptical? I just want to repair things with you. Step by step we can forgive each other. What do you say, truce?"

"Okay but you have to promise not to say anything negative the entire time we are together. Maybe this weekend we can go to Bayshore Mall and then eat at the Cheesecake Factory."

"Sounds like a plan to me baby girl. I hope all has been well your way lately." I couldn't believe how calm we both remained which was a big step in itself. Our conversation lasted a few more minutes until Juanita beeped in.

"Hey Nita, girl. I was on the other line with Tia. We had a productive chat and plan to hang out the weekend."

"Oh wow! That is great to hear. You two are so much alike and I pray your relationship grows. I didn't want anything girl, just to say hey. I'm about to go to this concert with Martin. I pray I'm home before midnight. You know I'm usually in bed by ten o' clock."

"I'm already in the bed, chile. With a book in hand. Enjoy and be safe."

"Alright, call you tomorrow. Night," she said then hung up.

I let out a few chuckles then proceeded to read a few more chapters of the newest book in my collection before lights out. *The Other Side of the Pastors Bed's* by Kala Andre wasn't something I should've read before bed because I tossed and turned half the night. I dreamed Charles cheated on me with Angela and everyone at church knew about it. Also, Tia taunted me and helped Angela kick me out of my house. Finally, at four o'clock I climbed out of bed and went downstairs to make coffee. I turned on the television and scanned to MSNBC until Morning Joe came on at five.

By seven, I was frying bacon. I placed medium sized pancakes on a plate, and the eggs hit the pan. Charles came down first, fully dressed in a black Sean John suit looking like a freshly trimmed model. Umm, he was so freaking sexy with his salt n pepper beard. "Morning husband. How'd you sleep?" I asked in a sarcastic tone, but I don't believe he picked it up.

"Like a baby, actually, but I noticed you didn't. What's wrong?"

"Bad dreams. I'll get a nap once you and the girls leave." In walked the girls, who were dressed already too. "Morning baby girls. You two look refreshed and ready to start the day off right. Sit down and eat before you dart out of this house."

"Morning Mama, morning Daddy," they said sitting at the table wasting no time tearing up their food before rushing out to school.

"Okay, baby. Have a great day, pray, and keep spreading the good news! Remember you were given another day because someone needs your help. I'm going to shower and nap for a bit," I announced.

"Love you, Honey! Call me if you need anything. I hope to be home before ten tonight. I wish it was certain how long, but you know the routine."

With two pillows fluffed and placed behind my head and back, I continued the book further, implementing more paranoia. The character, Pastor Martin Sr., was a pure trip, going so far as to having sex in the church. As I kept reading and reading I found myself sipping wine, wondering if a pop-up visit to Calvary was in order. I shook my head at the silly thought. Charles would never do anything like that--ever.

CHAPTER 15

ia Wallace

Whenever I woke up before the alarm it seemed my day always went well. The call from my mom last night and dinner with dad sort of made some of the anger escape my body. To get the morning started I decided to get up and go to the gym before having breakfast. Frequenting the gym helped tone the body and released negative vibes weighing on me. On the way home, a pit-stop for two things at Walmart costed me fifty dollars. It was hard to go in and not come out with more than one bag.

While I ate scrambled cheese eggs, bacon, and mini bagels, I contemplated about my life and what type of goals I needed to set. The dancing life had begun to get boring indicating time for a change. Plus, I had so much money stacked I didn't need to dance anymore.

As a work in progress, changes in my life were necessary in order to live freely. Step by step I was on a mission to be more family oriented and spend more time with my sisters. Things with Lance were moving in a positive direction, therefore I decided to invite him to Thanksgiving dinner. On the last piece of bacon, my phone rang and it was a number not recognizable. It was still early so I figured it was someone from the school.

"Hello?"

"What's up, Stranger? I'll give you two guesses on who this is."

"When the voice spoke, and it wasn't a white person, my flip lip took over. I'm too grown for guessing games so reveal yourself or get the dial tone."

"Damn girl you still snappy and straightforward with your mean ass. It's Eli, your old partner in crime."

"Wow, Eli. I haven't spoken to you in a very long time. How is life treating ya these days?"

"Life is good! I own my own business so a nigga stays busy. Aye, I heard you a professor now. How did that happen?"

"Ha, I know right. Hold on, how did you... My sister," she answered her own question as we laughed.

"Yeah, I went to church with my dad just, so I could find her to get to you. I accomplished that mission. We should meet up to chat face to face. I bet you're even more gorgeous than before."

"Umm, yeah we can do that. You still blow back?"

"I keep smoke, girl; ain't nothing changed. Actually, I was about to go blow one with Leon. Wanna meet me there? I understand if not."

"Yeah might as well, just finished breakfast too. Give me a minute to get dressed."

"Cool. Just text this number when you on the way then I'll meet you at the old spot."

"Bet."

Our lines disconnected, and I had the biggest grin. Wow. I haven't seen Leon since he tried to make a move on me, but once I set him straight we ended our friendship on good terms. I cleaned the kitchen then got dressed and headed out. It was still chilly outside so I wore a pair of slim grey dress pants, long-sleeved black top, and black flats. My hair was slicked back into a ponytail with a jacket. I was sexy in anything I wore but this time I tried to dress down.

* * *

I CRUISED DOWN 27th Burleigh headed to Leon's Sweet Spot. That was our spot back in the day when we wanted to chill and smoke low key. The owner of the place was a childhood friend we got our weed from. All we had to do in return was bring him business. I had a few boys back then who smoked all day every day; Leon made a lot of money off of them. He liked me, but he was married so he never pursued. Honestly, I believe Eli threatened him or something.

Two cars were already parked in the lot when I arrived. Besides a paint job, the Sweet Spot still looked the same. By the time I turned the engine off the two men who had become strangers appeared. Appearances alone, Eli was a fine piece of specimen. His face triggered memories causing me to grin as I exited the vehicle.

"Aye what up T-Dawg," Leon said with his arms wide open ready to embrace me. I gave him a quick hug and turned my attention to Eli. We hugged and during that time the smell of his Calvin Klein made me not want to let go.

"Hey, it's been way too long. Dude, you still look the same just muscular." The three of us walked inside to catch up and laugh about the good old days we shared.

"Ha, I was going to say the same thing. Girl you fine as hell. Where are you living at nowadays?"

"An hour away from my parents' house. I'm kind of scared to move anywhere else at the moment. Although the Midwest seems to be my best bet if I do relocate."

"I live in Illinois. Keeping my business running is hard damn work. Owning and managing a business required focus, money, and time. I stay away for that purpose. What about you and the whole professor thang?" he teased. Lauren couldn't hold water with her blabbermouth. She told Eli all my updates except the dancer gig.

"Yeah, one day I applied for some assistant positions until one day a permanent position opened up to teach freshmen students. Without anything to lose, teaching seemed like a good way to give back. I believe it's my duty to invest in the students who are our future."

"That's dope. I'm sure the students appreciate you, huh? Especially them mannish young guys."

"I sure hope they do! The boys don't be all googly-eyed anymore but during the first week, a few tried me. Now, they just think I'm a cool professor who doesn't play that foolishness."

"Cool, T. I'm proud you! How is the rest of your fam? Aye, yo mama saw me at church talking to your sister and walked right over to us too."

"Yeah, she ain't changed much, sad to tell you. We've been going at it again but we're trying to work through our issues."

"Women," Leon mumbled then laughed before he disappeared upstairs to finishing prepping to open for the day. That was my cue to get out of there too only because I couldn't trust myself alone with Eli. Chilling with Eli and Leon took me back to my teenage days when we used to be wild. Eli was my only male friend who didn't try to push up on me. We helped each other out when our parents nagged us.

Eli came back into my life at the wrong time and it sucked so badly because I was in love with him. The old feelings and memories from our teen days clouded my judgment. Maybe he's the man I was supposed to really be with instead of Lance. He was the black sheep and son of Deacon Brown from my father's church. Back in the day growing up, we hung together the majority of the time because we were so much alike; the bad seeds of the bunch.

The rest of the week went by fairly quickly as the students occupied most of my time with projects and one-on-one meetings. I'll admit hearing from Eli made my body tingle inside but my relationship with Lance was a good thing. Sometimes God doesn't allow certain unions to form because it was not meant to be. The week ended on a good note and I prayed the happy streak that hovered over me would continue into the weekend.

* * *

I MADE it to Bayshore Mall right before noon, only to notice my mother three cars down. I yelled out to her waving my hand as I walked in the direction she stood until we were close enough to hug. Refreshed, seeing my mother was almost a delight because for the first time in a long time, I needed her advice on something personal. Our lunch at Devon's Seafood and Steak was on point. Small talk between us two got more comfortable over time to the point I opened up a little bit.

During our conversation, I realized that Queen deserved a phone call and apology from me. Not talking to her was a big mistake and if I could forgive my mom, I had to forgive her too. Stubborn, I never liked to hear anyone tell me what to do even if it was the truth. A best friend was supposed to be completely honest--Queen was that friend. I made a mental note to call her when I got home.

My mother and I shopped together, something we hadn't done in so long it felt foreign. Her sense of humor never faded giving us something to break the ice. In that moment, I wished my sisters were with us because it was the perfect family moment. Nevertheless, one-on-one time was much needed. My father wanted peace therefore I obliged and I'm glad to have put my stubborn ways aside. I texted her when I made it home.

Afterwards, my pride allowed me to call Queen to apologize and make peace. A friendship like ours was too important for pettiness. It amazed me how petty women could be and would let pride jack up a bond. Going without talking or seeing each other only made me miss her more. At the end of our conversation, life was so much better. A productive day caused for a nice joint and a good laugh at the show Blackish to end the night.

I was so busy grading papers and midterms daily that the end of the week crept up fast, giving me a reason to look forward to the weekend. At my desk on a Friday afternoon, my wrists began to ache which was clearly a sign to leave. In the midst of straightening the papers on my desk, the vibration of my phone caught my ear. Out of all folks it was Nadia, she probably wondered what the heck happened to me. I hadn't been to the club in a long time and had plans to quit. Her message served as a reminder to go see Chastity. I grabbed my phone and shot her a message back.

Me: Hey chick! I'm coming to the club tonight but not to work. I'll fill you in later before you hit the stage.

Three gray dots appeared letting me know she was typing back. I gathered my bags locked my office and read her message in the car. I went home long enough to eat then change into jeans before going back out for a few hours. During the drive, life's events flashed through my head. I prayed Chastity didn't give me hell as I climbed out my ride with my Gucci bag and strutted to the door. I walked through the entrance and went straight to Chastity's office located a few doors down from the dressing room. I tapped on her door three times and waited for her to answer.

"Who the hell is it?" Her muffled voice projected through.

"It's Coco. I really need to talk to you," I yelled back shifting my weight from leg to leg while I waited.

She snatched the door open to invite me in and went back to sit at her desk. It wasn't certain if she was in a bad mood or not so I eased into the conversation. *What could she do to me for quitting? Nothing,* I said silently to myself. "Well Chastity I wanted to thank you for--," she cut me off instantly.

"Chile, you about to tell me you quit, right? You ain't the first or the last so don't beat around the bush. I'm glad you found something better."

"Yes. It's time to hang up the G-string and focus on my future. I'll admit it was a fun ride." I unzipped my bag and removed two hundred dollar bills from my wallet and placed them on her desk. "This is to say thank you for giving me a chance."

"You alright with me Coco," she said as she slipped the money off the desk and into her pocket. In return we shared a joint and then I went to find Nakia before I left for good.

CHAPTER 16

$\mathcal{C}$onnie Wallace

During my drive to Bayshore Mall, a Joyce Meyer's audiobook played; giving me courage and strength. My husband said some stuff that wouldn't escape me only because his words were true. Going to meet Tia for lunch was a big step for both of us and by the grace of God, I prayed for peace. Just as I pulled into a parking spot and exited my vehicle, my daughter's voice gained my attention as she approached.

"Hi Honey. So glad to see you!" I leaned in and kissed her on the cheek. Still in a calm state, we embraced and I'll admit it felt great. The love I had for that child was beyond measurable, but her attitude was too much.

"Hey Mama, good to see you as well! How ya been? Dad said yall went to Atlanta."

"Chile, you know me, busy with the women's ministry and keeping up with your father. I've even taken up yoga. Our trip to Atlanta was wonderful and your father did his thing as guest pastor. We even had some alone time." Side by side we walked and talked, before I knew it we were in front of Devon Seafood and Steak.

"Glad you are trying yoga, it should lower your anxiety and stress."

"Maybe we could try it together, you just might enjoy it. Your father believes it would be a step towards mending our dysfunctional relationship."

"Baby steps mom, let's get through today before we start planning BFF dates. Sorry if that was too flip at the lip."

Without a reply to Tia, I smiled as we were greeted immediately upon entering the restaurant. Our waiter was a fairly young white guy who was very attractive, to say the least. Almost forgot I was the pastor's wife for a quick second.

"Good afternoon ladies, welcome to Devon. Will there just be the two of you?"

"Yes!" Tia answered as if she was smitten by his appearance too.

"Follow me this way, I'll get you two a seated away from the doors."

Never had I dated outside my race, but it was a true curiosity of mine about dating a white man. The waiter left us to get situated and to scan the menu. While scanning the menu several items caught my taste buds. I had to make sure not to stick my tongue out too far.

"Order whatever you want Honey, it's on me today. Chile, my stomach flipping right now I'm so hungry."

"Me too. Oh! I see crab cakes and calamari, that's what I'm getting."

"So, what's new since the last time we saw each other? School going well?" I wanted Tia to know my interest in her life was important to me. I really prayed she saw my push to be a better parent. Although grown, she was old enough to know parents aren't perfect.

"Actually, everything is going well with school and life in general. The students have shown growth in their manners, understanding the material, and adapting to college. I'm seeing someone as well and it might be serious."

"That is good to hear, Honey! It means you are doing your job the correct way and making an impact on them. I'm proud of you for that. As for the guy you're seeing, keep those details until you're ready to share."

"That was my plan anyway," she said then chuckled. I shook my head and chuckled too because she was so quick with her tongue.

"Okay, mom, I need your advice on something but cannot give you details because it's something you don't need to know about. There is a friend who does something very risky for her job and will not listen to advice given by her good girlfriend. The women are all stubborn and have pride issues. What do you suggest they do so that friendship can be fun again?"

"First off, friends will have disagreements and argue but real friends will apologize to each other. The only thing I can suggest is to pray, reach out, and know the things you did to make amends. Sometimes it will take a hard fall for the lesson to be learned."

"Well said, mother dear. Thank you!"

"Alright, let's go do a little shopping before we split for the day!"

* * *

AFTER A LOVELY MEAL, Tia and I walked to Bath & Body Works and Charlotte Russe. I found myself laughing so hard at the things my daughter said as she shared stories from work with her students. Life as a professor seemed to make her beyond happy. Charles was right, our daughter had some good qualities. Her dedication to the students was impressive. I was truly proud of her actions to help them succeed.

"Tia, do you need a winter coat?" My question might have seemed awkward given she was a grown woman.

"Really Mom?"

"What? You are still my child. Besides, your dad will foot the bill." We had just entered Boston Store when I spotted a soft pink asymmetrical zip coat on sale. It was for reasons like this I had a secret Boston Store credit card.

"That is cute Mom. You should get it if that's what you want." I noticed her scanning through the rack of fur hood coats. The white and black faux fur asymmetrical zip puffer jacket held her attention the most.

"Get it," I insisted not taking no for an answer either. She took the coat off the rack doing her best not to cheese hard. We walked to the nearest register to get rung up before going our separate ways. With two bags apiece, we made our exit out the store and back to our vehicles. "Tia, I really had a good time today hanging out with you. In all seriousness, we need to do this more often; with baby steps of course. I had some time to think while in Atlanta and I know as a mother you will never understand some of the things I've done. Nevertheless, you are my daughter and I love you, Honey."

"Today was pretty dope I'll admit. Sometimes my mouth gets in the way which causes drama but I'm a work in progress. God ain't done with me yet, Mama. I'm sorry and plan to do better. Who knows yoga might be worth looking into next if it's helping you that much."

"Okay baby girl, let me get my butt home. Please call or text me when you make it home." For the first time in a long time, Tia and I shared a hug, not just a hug, one that was an assurance that things were going to be alright.

"Alright, Mama. Love you! Tell everyone I said hello." I watched her get into her car first then I followed suit as I strapped on my seatbelt. With one tap of a button, Kimberla Lawson Roby's audiobook guided my smooth ride home. Charles wasn't there yet--go figure--leaving me a little down time before focusing my attention on church-related tasks. I quickly shot Tia a text so she knew I made it safely. She sent one shortly afterward putting a smile on my face.

CHAPTER 17

Queenetta "Queen" Jones

It had been a few days since Tia and I had a major blow up about her giving up the exotic dancing life. She had become so immersed in the life that she didn't realize how it affected her. I loved my friend and only wanted the best for her. Saturday night she invited me to the lounge. As soon as my singles disappeared in the G-string of a strapped redbone chick, my boredom grew. Minutes later commotion started, security rushed over to subdue an angry customer.

The incident that happened at work and I feared for her safety. A crazy customer tried to get rough by grabbing her until security snatched his ass up. She tried to play it off as if she didn't get scared or it wasn't a big deal. The only reason I didn't take further actions is because I blamed myself for daring Tia to become a dancer but not more than I blame Nakia. Chilling back watching the TV show *Power* I scrolled through my contacts until I found the number. With a few strokes of the keys, a message was sent to Nakia indicating we needed to meet up in person.

Morning wake n bake was something every smoker took part in to help them function and tackle their day. Same with me. I smoked to get high, for relaxation and because it was better than hardcore drugs. Half a blunt gave me the munchies and urge to call my best friend. She had been avoiding my calls, but I figured she slept her attitude away and would answer. When I called her the phone rung at least four times before her voicemail kicked on.

"Tia, I don't know if you screening calls or not, but we need to talk —ASAP--because we been friends too long. You can be stubborn but, what I said to you was strictly out of love. I'm trying to give you a little space, but please believe I will do a pop-up visit. Call me back." That was the second message I'd left and she ignored me.

Tired of reaching out to miss stubborn ass, she would come around sooner than later. For the next few hours, I prepped for work hoping my eight hours flew by fast. My job at the DISH Network Company had grown to be a little boring despite how nice the people were. It was then I decided to search for other options for employment, it was a job out there somewhere for me.

Soon as I punched the time clock, there was a list of tasks on my desk. There were ten items that took at least five hours to complete, so the crew teamed up to get them done. As a supervisor, I gave orders to the men employees, who didn't seem to have a problem with a female calling shots. Each person pulled their weight making time fly. We made the job fun but made sure things were done correctly.

During inventory count, Nate assisted me to serve as an extra pair of hands which was appreciated. He was professional at all times, but occasionally slipped up and said or did something that could've been considered inappropriate. Since he was eye candy I never reported him. Besides, if I felt threatened or uncomfortable I was bold enough to call him out. Once our tasks were completed, the last three hours of my shift consisted of entering information into a spreadsheet. When the vibration of my Fitbit went off I knew it was quitting time. The crew made sure the shop was in order before we closed up and left the premises. To ensure I made it to my car, the guys tended to escort me and watched me drive off. Going straight home, everything I needed was there giving me no reason to make any stops along the way. Like clockwork, I undressed, showered, ate and smoked while I watched Shameless on Netflix.

* * *

JUST AS I nodded out my cell kept vibrating leaving me curious who it was calling. When I flipped the phone over to scan the screen, Tia appeared. I let out a deep sigh hoping she wasn't about to start trouble. "Hello," I answered in a dry voice.

"Queen I'm calling to say I'm sorry! You tried to be a friend and provide constructive criticism. I had time to think about what you said, and you were right. My mom made me realize that I was acting immature. Please forgive me."

"Your mom? Y'all done made up?"

"We are working on it. We spent the day together at the mall and it was honestly refreshing. So, you see I'm making amends with those I care about. Huh, I'm even meeting my dad for dinner Monday. He rearranged his day for me."

"Wow, that is a big step for all of you! I forgive you and I'm proud that you got your mind right. All of us care about your big head ass. What's been new your way?"

"Working with those darn students and getting used to being with a man. Lance has been great and has gotten on my tail about quitting the club too. Needless to say, that job is over."

"Best friend, I was the one who dared you to do it so in my head it was only right for me to talk you away from the place. Think about it from my point of view, you would feel a little guilty too. Anyway, I'm glad we are talking again Ms. Don't Tell Me Nothing."

"It's all good! Like my mom said, real friends will always forgive and make up."

"Damn, yo mama really turning over a new leaf and it ain't even the New Year yet. God is working on her."

"Too good to be true right? Well, I need to get myself ready for bed but had to call you. Can't wait to get together soon to catch up. Love you BFF," I said before ending the call. Before Tia called I was just about to get settled. It was nice Tia's parents wanted to show their efforts and interest in building their relationship. I swear my friend had two blessings I'd give anything to have but, my grandma was perfect enough.

CHAPTER 18

*P*astor Charles Wallace

Every morning I thanked the Lord for another opportunity to be great. Each day went by fast and it amazed me how quickly Saturday and Sunday came around. Twenty-four hours just wasn't enough time in a day to accomplish things. As Thanksgiving approached, much needed work had to be done. Our partnering churches had begun to have boxes of food delivered for the less fortunate families. It amazed me how fast November had come.

Saturday night while Connie helped me polish up the sermon, she told me about her afternoon with Tia. I watched her face glow as she talked about shopping for a winter coat and how they laughed with each other. Amazed at how much change Connie had undergone in little time made me proud as a husband. A few minor edits later and the sermon was ready for the morning. The next day Sunday service went as planned and we gained five new members in the process. All five were siblings who wanted to get involved in church instead of running the streets. Calvary's membership had been steadily increasing and I was glad.

Sunday evening, I completed a few tasks that I typically did Monday evening. I called Tia to make sure we were still on for dinner and proceeded with the reservations at the Capital Grille. It was important that our bond became stronger. The strip club scene drove a wedge between us and I wanted to fix it. I spent the rest of Sunday and Monday afternoon occupied with meetings both in person and by telephone. As a pastor it was important to make connections with the community, partnering churches, and of course law enforcement.

* * *

INDEPENDENT like always Tia insisted on driving herself which was okay with me. All I cared about was catching up and of course to be nosey. I arrived a few minutes early at the Capital Grille parking directly in front. Inside, our seats were located in the middle of the room in a cozy booth. I took the liberty to place our food orders while I waited for Tia. I silenced my phone so there were distractions or interruptions during our meal. I was a firm believer that phones shouldn't be allowed at the table.

"Hey, Daddy," her voice hit my ears prompting me to stand.

"There she goes, my baby girl! Give me a hug." We embraced as my hug lasted longer than it should. Excited to see her, my wide smile from ear to ear was proof as we sat down together. "So, your mom told me you two had a great time over the weekend. Thank you for giving her another chance."

"Yes. Things went better than expected and I truly had fun. She didn't pry into my business nor did she make a bunch of off the wall comments. Hey, we both are a work in progress. God ain't done with me yet."

"Same here. We all are a work in progress, Honey. I hope you don't mind that I ordered already. I'm positive you'll enjoy."

"Oh, my goodness! Daddy, you didn't. What did you order?" Just as she asked, the waitress came out with our appetizers and beverages. She sat the Caesar salad and pan-fried calamari in front of Tia. When she licked her lips, I knew my choices were correct. I was allergic to seafood so, I ordered French onion soup.

"I ordered us 14 oz. New York style steaks with asparagus and garlic mashed potatoes for the main course. While we wait I want to talk about something important."

"Dad if it's about that night, please leave it alone. That was such an embarrassing moment for us both--let it stay in the past. Besides, why ruin a perfect father and daughter night. All is forgiven as long as it remains between us two."

"Tia, you just don't understand how bad I felt about the whole situation but like you said, I'm willing to leave it all in the past. Let's make a toast to a new beginning!" She raised her water glass to mine in recognition of a fresh start. No father wanted a torn or strained relationship with their child. In my case, Tia was a grown woman, so I couldn't force her to talk to me. Our time together was a success and I won't lie, the weight from my shoulders were lifted. By the time I made it home Connie had waited up just to hear the details of the evening.

* * *

TUESDAYS USED to be days I dreaded but since Angela and I had been slipping around; it had become the best day of the week. Our extracurricular activities were wrong. Committing adultery was never something I planned. Each time I tried to break it off, her soul-sucking eyes put me in a love trance. Angela was the opposite of Connie and made me feel special in a sexual way. She was in a sorority, driven, and did some things with her mouth that should have been illegal. After the deacon board meeting, everyone was dismissed, and I gave Angela enough time to leave first.

I arrived at her home per my usual routine on Tuesday evenings. Daylight savings time made my visits unnoticed in the darkness. On the porch, the door opened. "Come right in, Lova Man." She pulled me inside by the collar of my shirt.

"Wow!" Angela had changed out of her navy blue pants suit to a silk robe with no underwear. Before I got too comfortable I sent the preset text message to Connie.

Me: Hey honey! I don't think I will be able to make it to dinner tonight. Got tied up in some paperwork. Will be home before midnight. Love You! CW

Once the message sent my finger flipped the side button to vibrate then I hung up my coat. Before I knew it one thing led to another and Angela's legs occupied my hands. I rubbed cocoa butter lotion on them. How did I let the devil get a hold of me again? This woman possessed me to do what she wanted me to do. My marriage had been reduced to lies as I sinned with another woman. A Christian man of God, but my actions lately resembled those of a man who let my bad choices affect my family.

"Wow Charles, how can sin feel so good right now? You were amazing just now. How much longer can we keep doing this? I'm beginning to catch feelings; feelings I shouldn't experience."

"Our actions will have consequences but right now I'm loving every minute with you. Eventually we have to break things off but not now. There was a time when this moment with you was a fantasy, now here we are in each other's arms. I'll have to leave soon."

"Can we just lay here a little while longer? I just want to feel your warm body up against mine. Our time is already limited not to mention the extra precautions we must go through." Angela made me not want to go home, but I knew that was no option especially since I missed dinner. I laid with Angela another ten minutes before I hopped up to freshen up. Angela bought me some non-fragrance soap for my man parts to avoid suspicions from Connie.

CHAPTER 19

Lauren Wallace

It had been close to three weeks and no period, yet which had me freaking the hell out. There was no way I could be pregnant because we used protection; made sure to be extra careful. Neither my parents nor Azriah's would be happy about a baby born out of wedlock. My father's reputation was everything, so my situation would cause gossip, which was the last thing I wanted to happen. Before blabbing my mouth, this secret remained quiet until it was a for sure thing. Unable to focus, my day was thrown off at work with thoughts of pregnancy, how to tell everyone, and if college was possible.

Hesitant to go downstairs for dinner, my mom made four-cheese lasagna, garlic bread, and Caesar salad. The garlic bread smell alone made my stomach loudly growl as my mouth watered. Food was my best friend and my plate was proof.

"Lauren, you need to watch your weight honey; you're going to turn into a chubby girl."

"Wow, Mom, you are such a self-esteem killer. I'm not even chubby."

"Exactly. Let's keep it that way. You must learn to proportion your food, so you can live a long healthy life. I look forward to grandchildren when the time is right of course."

Without a word, I stuffed bread in my mouth but couldn't help to notice my mama side eyeing me. She indirectly stared at me as if she knew I was hiding something. Without another word, my fork moved from the plate to my mouth until the dish was empty. I believed mothers had a special gene that allowed them to detect when their child lies or is up to something. Just when I thought the evening was over, my father asked me about college.

"You must be excited to attend Spelman in August? Baby girl, you are going to fall in love with the school and the hospitality everyone shows."

"Yes, very much so Daddy!"

"Have you decided on a major yet?"

"No Daddy. No major yet, but a minor in writing for sure. I'm still undecided on the majors because there are so many."

"Whatever you decide to do, do it for you and not to please your mother and me. We had our college days. It's only fair you create your own. However, remember the legacy; you will be the fourth generation Wallace to carry the name on campus."

"Yes, sir. I won't let you down," the words rolled from mouth knowing I was possibly pregnant. Shockingly my mother kept quiet the entire time without as much as an utter.

"Umm... sorry to interrupt, but may I be excused, please? I have to clean the kitchen and finish the last of my homework," Gabby explained.

"Yes, Honey, go right ahead," mama gave permission to proceed.

"Ahh me too. I need to shower then prep for work." I removed myself from the seat and walked into the kitchen to load my plate in the dishwasher. From there I went straight upstairs to my room for a shower. The entire room smelled like strawberries from the body wash and shampoo I used daily. With the fan on in the bathroom, the sweet smell soothed me as I applied lotion to my body. The benefit of having your own room is being able to wear panties and a shirt to bed.

There was never a time I ever wished my period would come down more than right now. Still stuck with the possibility of being with child, Tia was the only person I felt comfortable enough to tell. I'm confused on how it happened because my eyes watched Azriah put on a condom. I finally got the nerves to text my sister and within minutes she FaceTime me.

"Damn sis, what the heck is going on with you? If it's been this long you probably are knocked up. Pray aunt flow come to visit in the next three days or mama will have a heart attack."

"Oh gosh, Tia, what am I going to do? Dad is gonna flip his wig but I'm more afraid of Mommy Dearest."

"Hum… We will get through this no matter what; it is your body, your life. I'm in your corner. Tell you what, when I come for dinner Sunday I will bring three pregnancy tests. Before the night is over we will figure out a plan on what your options are."

"Okay. Thanks Sis for calming me. This is so scary. Please don't tell Queen or anyone else."

"This is our secret, Sissy. Until then do your best to stay out of mom's sight so she has no reason to fuss. I'm about to grub on pizza and grade papers. Get some rest and be cool. I love you, girl." Tia blew a kiss before we disconnected the line. Flat on my back, I lay in bed thinking when the vibrations from my phone broke my train of thought. It was Azriah calling, quickly my finger hit the ignore button, not ready to talk to him yet. Persistent, he followed up with a text message, so I replied so he wouldn't call again.

ME: Hey you! I missed your call, stepped away from the phone for a sec. What are you up to?

AB: Thinking of you lovely woman! Ready to be with you for a while. I can't wait to go off to college; more freedom to live like an adult. It sucks we have to slip around behind our parents' back.

ME: It sure does suck but that is what makes it all so fun!

AB: True. What are doing right now?

ME: Bored. Sad. Missing you.

AB: Meet me at the back door at ten-thirty. Need to see you before I go to sleep.

* * *

"OH SHIT! I have to get out of here," Azriah shouted.

His sudden jump up from the bed woke me. He slipped on his shirt and shoes. I snuck him in last night for a few hours and ended up falling asleep together. The last thing I can recall, he talked about the future after college. Close to seven o'clock, the sun was out already. He was about to open the door, but I quickly stopped him.

"Dude, hold on. Let me do a walk through first to see where everyone is at before you slip out. Hold tight for a few minutes."

"Damn, girl you gonna get us in trouble. Hurry up," he insisted as he paced back and forth.

"Okay, I'll be right back. Don't come out until then." I walked slowly down the stairs as I listened to my parents' voices. Swiftly I went back up to let Azriah out of the bedroom and out the back exit. A sigh of relief escaped my body once he left. He was still unaware of the possible pregnancy, it had to be the right time though.

* * *

THANKSGIVING WAS one of my favorite holidays because of the feast but also because I had a chance to make a difference. Every year our family served food to the homeless and those who were less fortunate. A lot of people fell on tough times with the loss of loved ones, no home, or no family. The holiday fell on a Thursday, so we served a feast style meal that Wednesday evening and late Thursday morning. The church mothers along with other volunteers cooked for almost eight hundred people. Everybody worked in shifts to serve. My family served for at least three hours before departing home.

I was glad my mom and Gabby cooked most of our food already. I tried to stay out of sight as much as possible. Best Buy had the nerve to make me work but my vomiting got me sent home early. When I made it home I noticed Tia's car in the driveway making me smile. In perfect timing, I made it inside to meet Lance, Tia's new boyfriend. Selfishly, I prayed all of the attention would be on Tia and her white chocolate man.

abrielle Wallace

The night before Thanksgiving my mom made me pick collard greens, cut sweet potatoes for pies and potatoes for potato salad. Time in the kitchen together made our bond strong and memorable; something I wished my sisters could have shared. There was a fun maternal side Tia never saw in our mother. Cooking was her passion, it brought her peace too. As the last child of the bunch, there were qualities in my mom I saw that made me feel differently than my sisters. That was the main reason I couldn't reveal to her my preference for girls.

My mom hit the oven button on the stove. "Gabby get those pie shells and carton of eggs from the refrigerator. While I do the pies, I need you to wash the greens and put them in the two silver pots. Make sure the water is boiling really well before you put them in, the ham hocks will become tender and add flavor."

"Yes, ma'am!" I moved around the kitchen over to the sink where the two silver pots were located. I cleaned then filled one side of the sink with water and dumped the greens inside. As I washed them I moved them into the empty jumbo pan, I repeated the process once again. The smell if the ham hocks seeped into the air. I added the greens into the pots. The oven beeped as I opened the door and moved out the way. My mom slowly slid the rectangle pan with two egg pies down on the second rack. She then slid another pan with two sweet potato pies on the top rack. Gently closing the door, she proceeded to prep.

Most of the food was cooked the night before so that our family could serve God's children at church. Spending three to five hours serving those less fortunate made me grateful. When we got back home I washed up and headed back to the kitchen with my mother. The last items were potato salad and macaroni. Four eggs boiled in a small pot while I continuously stirred the mac noodles and white potatoes on the back eye. Once the eggs were ready I removed them from the heat to the sink for peeling. Then I poured the noodles through the strainer, but my mom moved in to take care of it.

"I'll do this honey. No offense but this must be cheesy and creamy so I'm using Velveeta cheese instead of American slices." We shared a laugh as I whipped up the potato salad. I sprinkled an even amount of paprika over it then covered it and stuck it in the refrigerator for a few minutes to chill.

* * *

WHEN THE TABLE was officially set, each dish sat with a big plastic spoon inside. The variety ranged from fluffy dressing, collard greens, candy yams, ham, macaroni and cheese, potato salad, spaghetti, corn muffins, sweet potato pies and Louisiana Crunch Cake. The Lord blessed my mother's hands; I couldn't wait to taste every single dish. I went upstairs, quickly freshened up and change clothes. At my mom's request, I slipped into a grey sweater dress with long sleeves. She disliked me wearing pants because she felt young girls and women should only wear dresses. I slithered my feet inside the open toe black one-inch heels. With a lite strut, I went down each stair careful not to bust my butt. Heels weren't my favorite, but I had to learn to walk in them.

The front door opened just as I moved out the way. "Hey, Sissy." I gave Tia a big hug and kiss on the cheek. She had a charming looking guy with her. He was a surprise guest. My sister knew how to shake stuff up; she knew darn well our mama didn't know how to behave during dinner. I extended my hand out to shake his as Tia introduced us to each other.

"Oh, um, shoes off please."

The minute the three of us popped our heads in the kitchen my mother's face let me know she was about to be petty. Her forehead wrinkled for a second then her fake smile appeared. The last thing she expected was a white dude strolling through her kitchen. Moving closer to them she kept the phony smile before finally speaking.

"Hello, I'm Tia's mother. I wasn't aware my daughter had a plus one, but you are more than welcomed. Gabby, please set another place at the table."

"Yes ma'am," I replied not moving a muscle.

"Hi, Mrs. Wallace it's really nice to finally meet you, ma'am! I'm Lance. Thank you for accepting me for dinner."

"So how do you know my daughter?"

That is when Tia tried to interrupt *"Ahem,"* as she cleared her throat in an effort to avoid his answer. With a smile, I just waited and listened to see how long the interrogation would go on. In the meantime, Lauren came through the door joining in on the excitement.

"I'm here family! Hey sis," she hugged me then Tia while she gave Lance a semi-side eye. She proceeded to grill him herself with a few questions. "Hi, are you one of my sister's students? You are a cute piece of white chocolate."

"Lauren, stop it. You know better girl," my mother interrupted.

"Thank you. We're about to sit in the front until it's time to eat. C'mon Lance." I set the table with the silverware, glasses, and cloth napkins making sure to include Lance. The dining room table was in close proximity to the sitting room and front entrance to the foyer. My dad walked through the door as Tia and Lance sat holding hands. Nosey by nature I observed his reaction to Tia and her new friend. I couldn't hear what was said between them, but the body language displayed a welcoming gesture. I prayed we would be able to gather as a happy family without yelling or drama. It was a long shot, but I had faith my mother would act civil given there was a guest in the midst.

"Before we dig in, let's go around the table and say what you are thankful for," my mom requested. She continued, "I'll start. I'm thankful for family and the ability to serve an awesome God." "Gabby, what about you?"

"Umm, I'm thankful for sisterhood, great parents, and for life," I answered proudly then turned to Lauren. It appeared that her mind was somewhere else because I had to call her name twice. "Lauren. Lauren, can you hear me?"

"W-what? Sorry. I'm thankful for family and for having the best sisters in the world. Tia, your turn."

"Every day is Thanksgiving! I'm thankful for life and for a new friendship." As the head of the table, my father gave thanks last.

"Dear heavenly Father, we thank you for this day of thanksgiving, and for each day you allow us to wake and continue your work. I want to thank you for family. Now let's eat up."

"So, Lance how did you and my daughter meet? On campus?"

"Uhh, no, we met at the lounge."

"The what?" My mother questioned in confusion.

"The club mom," Tia intervened as if she tried to keep Lance from saying more.

"For heaven's sake child, you still out here clubbing and carrying on? I swear you have so much potential for good, yet you sin without regret."

"CONNIE," my father spoke through gritted teeth in an effort get her to shut up. He had a disappointed and unhappy look and so did Tia, who wore a worried look on her face.

I tried to change topics to something else hopeful the mood at the table would turn. "Umm, did I mention that I received an email from Spelman to set up a college tour?" It remained quiet until surprisingly Lance spoke.

"Congratulations, that must be exciting."

"Thank you and yes, it is because I'm the fourth generation and I get the chance to explore Atlanta. I've never been outside of Wisconsin so I'm super excited. My sister will be there too."

"Wow, that means this house will be quiet, you must look forward to that Mr. Wallace," Lance joked.

"You know Lance; my girls haven't been much trouble in the house so it will be a difficult time when they move out. Also as a pastor my schedule keeps me pretty busy but traveling to visit my girls is something I will make time for."

Obviously, my mother had to put her two cents in and speak too. The moment she fixed her mouth to speak, my eyes glanced at Tia and Lauren. We all widen our eyes with a slight shake of the head. It was apparently more drama was on the way. I slide my dinner plate to the left of me and reach for a slice of sweet potato pie.

"Lance tell us something about yourself. Where did you go to school? What do you do for a living? That is if my daughter doesn't object."

"I attended UW-Madison on a scholarship for all four years before moving to Connecticut. There I attended Yale, School of Engineering and Applied Science. Today I'm co-founder of Instabook, at Tech Work Computer Company."

She looked impressed by his accomplishments and even cracked a partial smile to ensure him she was listening. Tia looked proud of him too as she watched more our father's reactions. In my honest opinion, he was cute and smart enough to be my sister's boyfriend.

"Well, I'm glad that you and my daughter had the chance to connect. Maybe you'll encourage her to be more of a homebody and put a ring on it. I would love grandkids someday."

"Mom," I hissed at her comment along with everyone else except Lance. He dismissed it with a lite chuckle but had no idea the drama that was about to take place. Without another word, I finished my food before I cut a huge piece of crunch cake. The show was about to begin, and I had a front-row seat. That is when Tia spoke out.

"It gets boring being the topic of discussion during every dinner. I know there are other folks at this table who have something to talk about," Tia stated as she raised the fork to her mouth.

"Connie, not the time or place dear."

"Don't Dad, I've had all I can take from her. What happened to making amends and you trying to be a better mother? Huh, I knew that was bull crap. It's obvious you don't hold your tongue on how you feel about me. Well, guess what, Lance met me at Landing Strip Lounge. I'm an exotic dancer! Ha, add that to your list of disappointments."

Tia had just dropped a bombshell and we were all stunned to hear what she had just confessed. Shocked, I took a deep breath and stood up. My heart was pounding a mile a minute as I spoke up. All eyes were on me. "Well since Tia confessed, I have something to share as well. I'm a lesbian and have been for a long time. I'm sorry mom and dad, but this is who I am so please accept it." My mom let out a gasp but remained quiet.

"Gabby, I accept you but why didn't you talk to us about this privately?"

"Honestly, Dad I wanted to for a long time but mom and Tia argue so much I just didn't want to add to the drama. Plus, everyone thinks I'm a saint like I'm not human or something. I didn't tell anyone out of fear of being disowned by my mom." When I said that everyone turned to look at my mother who hadn't made a peep. I assumed she was still shocked by the double whammy revealed. Before sitting down, a loud sigh escaped me and no longer did the weight of fear hold me down. What happened next was beyond unexpected. Lauren rose to her feet but before she could speak my mom shouted.

"For heaven's sake! What do you have to say, child? I'm sure it can't be worse than what your sisters announced."

"Actually, it is worse Mom. I'm...I'm pregnant."

My father interrupted, "OH THE HELL you're not!" before Lauren finished her statement. Just a few seconds ago he went from the cool calm parent to shouting like my mother. In disbelief, there was nothing for me to do but eat and observe the drama unfold.

"Jesus take the wheel! My children have been possessed by the devil!" my mother shouted as she threw both hands in the air.

"Mom I know you got something to share, we have all confessed our deepest secrets. Remember Luke 12:2 says nothing is covered up that will not be revealed, or hidden that will not be known. What have you covered up or lied about?"

All eyes turned to the lady of the house who obviously felt the pressure of us staring her down. She raised her eyebrows as if she was beyond fed up with Tia and her back talk. The two shared a stare down without blinking before the gloves came off.

"Little girl don't forget whose house you are in, not to mention-- I'm your mother. You will show me some respect. Do you understand?"

"You have to give respect to earn it mother dearest. Oh, and guess what? I will not set foot back in your house!" Tia shouted back.

Our dysfunctional family had unfolded right before my eyes on the day we were supposed to be giving thanks for each other. Poor Lance wasn't ready to be introduced to the family in this manner, but it was the Wallace way. If he continued to date Tia after this, he would easily be a cool brother-in-law.

"Lance I'm truly sorry you had to witness this, but this dinner is officially over. I need to deal with my family in private. Please help yourself to food on your way out the door."

"Come on Lance, let's get the hell out of this house. We don't need food to go," Tia snapped leaving him confused. She gave me a big hug and told me how proud she was that I came out the closet. The minute the front door closed I began to clear the table in order to avoid my parents.

"Lauren please go to your room until your mother and I can figure out what to do with you. You better believe I'll pay you a visit tomorrow once the Lord sends me a sign on how to handle you. Oh, feel free to warn your little boyfriend because he will have to deal with me tomorrow. I hope you two talked about marriage, no daughter of mine is going to be a baby mama."

From the kitchen, I heard my dad yelling at Lauren all the while my mother remained in her seat. I loaded the dishwasher and put the food into containers. The kitchen was clean and my feet hurt and I smelled like a soul food restaurant. Without a word, to my parents, I slipped upstairs to my bedroom for a fast soak and wash. I usually soaked then stood for a shower to rinse. Unlike most folks, I preferred to air dry rather than use a towel as I slung of the zebra striped shower cap.

* * *

THE NEXT MORNING when I woke up for a bathroom run, I decided to do a walk through the house. There was no noise, no food aroma, or even a sign anyone was home. I went back upstairs to knock on Lauren's door but when I twisted the knob she was nowhere in sight. Puzzled, the logical thing to do was call and text my dad to find out what was going on. To my surprise he didn't answer so I texted my sister.

Me: Sis where you at? I woke to find out I'm the only one in the house.

Lauren: Yeah, Sis. I'm out with Azriah looking for an apartment. I can't stay under the same roof with that woman. Besides, last night was an eye-opener for me.

Me: Last night got out of hand sis. What were the odds of all three of us spilling the tea? Dude, mama face was priceless; she didn't know if she should scream or shout cuss words.

Lauren: Ikr. Huh, she took it well enough not to fall out or have a darn heart attack. Aye sis, when you stood up to announce you were a lesbian, Ma turned up her wine glass in one guzzle.

Me: Well good luck on the search. I'm about to make breakfast and lounge around the house. I pray it stays quiet without incident. That is until Dad finds out you moving out. Don't worry I won't say anything. Love you!

Lauren: Right. See you later or not Lol. Love you too!

CHAPTER 21

Connie Wallace

In the master suite, I paced back and forth, beyond pissed at my girls and husband. When Tia said the words Landing Strip it was clear that Charles knew about Tia the entire time. Made me wonder if he had some little jezebel shaking all on him. Who the hell did Tia think she was to talk to me in that tone? "Whew, Lord, please give me the strength!" I shouted out loud as I undressed out of my red Lisa Rene dress, bra, and panties. Rather confront my husband, I stepped into the shower big enough to fit three people inside. When I twisted the knob, water burst through the three shower heads mounted above me. It didn't matter that my hair got wet, nor did I care if my hands turned wrinkled. Not able to enjoy my peace for long, I heard a voice call out for me.

"Connie! Connie are you in here? We need to talk about what happened tonight," Charles' voice echoed as he found me washing. Our shower was glass, so I couldn't hide. He took a seat on the pure white stool that sat in the middle of the room. If I was in a mood for sex it would've been the perfect scene to set it off. I tried to ignore his glares as best I could, so he watched my backside most of the time.

Finally, I cut the water off and slide the glass door open. I stepped on the fuzzy rug that lay on the marble floor. He handed the bath towel to me and I quickly wrapped it around me.

"Hope that shower helped you figure out how we are going to repair our family. Can you believe one daughter is knocked up while the other likes girls? That goes to show how much attention we pay to our children."

"What do you want from me? According to Tia, I'm the one to blame for everything. At this point, it's your mess to clean."

"Are you mad, woman? This is our mess to clean. Oh, and yes you are partially to blame. Instead of always pointing out the bad in Tia, try praising the good. That is all she ever wanted from you. But you are too blinded to realize that."

"Wow, tell me how you really feel. Did you ever think that she blamed you for anything?" He had followed me back to our room as I applied lotion and stuff on my body before sliding on a pair of panties followed by silk pajamas.

"Blame me for what? I listen to her, praise her, and do my best to support her. Huh, did you forget that she's not even my biological daughter? Yet, I love her regardless."

"How dare you throw that in my face like that! It's not my fault I was in love with another man before I was promised to you. My mother's faults are not mine."

"Exactly, you can't treat Tia like your mom treated you. Tia deserves better especially since you have lied to her the entire time."

He was right, I had a tendency to put my foot in my mouth when it involved Tia, but she provoked me. Nevertheless, it gave me no reason to act out of character, but I lied for a reason. Joseph couldn't meet Tia, nor could she ever find out he was her father.

To avoid an argument with my husband, I went down to the kitchen to put water in the red tea kettle. It was the perfect time to do a little reading before calling it a night. Three of my favorite authors had just released books. I picked up my fully charged Kindle device to read Sins of My Beretta by author Trenae' from Lafayette, Louisiana.

Not your typical read for a pastor's wife, but these were the moments I looked forward to. Halfway through my eyes began to see doubles and I knew it was a matter of time before I crashed.

The next morning

I stayed in bed and played sleep the entire time. Charles moved around just to avoid talking to him about what happened last night. The moment I felt him lean over my body, I squeezed my eyes to ensure they remained closed. He placed a kiss on my forehead and whispered "I love you" before exiting the room. It wasn't until I heard his car pull off that I got out the bed to carry on with my day.

Showered and oiled down, I got dressed in a red skirt with off black stockings, a black Chiffon top, with bow earrings. With a short hairstyle, all it took was style comb and a few minutes to fluff my curls. I brushed my teeth and gargled before I applied a lite coat of Ruby Woo Mac lipstick. Back to the walk-in closet, I reach for a pair of Red Bottom pumps. My eyes spotted a black coat with ruffles the same length of my skirt. In the full-length body mirror, my outfit was the perfect look on a Friday morning. I switched items from my Gucci purse to a Chanel clutch as I did a double take then walked out of the house.

Inside Diamond, who was in need of a wash, the first stop I made was for a good hearty breakfast at Denny's downtown. Sandy, the waitress who waited on me twice a month, greeted me with a smile. She had a warming personality which is why I tipped her an extra twenty bucks no matter my bill. Eating healthy was important to me but sometimes the craving for bacon, eggs, and sausage caused me to indulge. Denny's was my spot, the place I felt like a regular person, not title or special treatment.

"Morning, Mrs. Wallace," she said seating me in the middle of the room.

"Thank you, Sandy. I'll have my regular, please."

She quickly brought me a water and orange juice and promised to have my food sooner than later. Patiently, I sat still finding myself gazing out the window. It was time to think about the direction of my life, how to deal with my girls and husband. The picture-perfect family the church thought existed in my household--was in shambles. Children are a reflection of their parents; therefore, it might appear that I failed as a mother, Charles a father. All in all, as a parent we do what we feel is right but sometimes that doesn't work. Parenting didn't come with a guidebook nor did my mother prepare me the proper way to be a mother. The more I sat and enjoyed my breakfast, the more I reflected on what I could do to make things better for me and my girls.

Charles hit the nail on the head when he told me I shouldn't treat my daughters how my mother treated me. It became clear how much my actions mirrored those of my controlling mom. Maybe counseling was best. Charles suggested repairing the broken bond with Tia. God was the only counselor I needed to mend and repair the mother-daughter bond.

To avoid being sluggish I walked and browsed through Nordstrom, not in search of anything specific. My plan wasn't to buy anything; I had gone over my spending limit for the month. Charles made it clear that money didn't grow on trees; he insisted that my spending limit remained at fifteen hundred dollars. In the middle of browsing, my phone made a chime sound. Without a thought, the phone stayed in my clutch because I assumed it wasn't important. It wasn't until an hour later that I decided to pull out my phone to check for missed calls. Like I figured no one called but there was a message on the phone screen. The number wasn't familiar to me at all.

Unknown: Meet me at Applebee's in Brookfield. We have something important to discuss. I'm sure you will want to see me. If you don't show, I will pop up at your nice fancy home. I'm sure you don't want that to happen.

Confused I pondered who would type such a message or even go as far to threaten to show up at my home. Unsure what to think I did what was logical; I went to Applebee's to find out who the mystery person was. I took off my Chanel designer sunglasses as a middle-aged hostess sat me in a booth towards the back of the restaurant. As much as I wanted to order an alcoholic beverage I ordered water with lemon and a chicken Caesar salad with extra dressing. I also ordered a grilled cheese sandwich with tomato soup. From my seat, my eyes scanned the entire place as I tried to spot anyone suspicious or a familiar face. Suddenly another message came through which made me jump a little.

Unknown: Wow! Your beauty has matured over time, yet I still get the same goosebump feelings I did over twenty years ago. Can you guess who I am now Connie?

I covered my mouth with my left hand in shock that Joseph, my high school sweetheart found me. A small lump formed in my throat as I looked around the place for him. His visit couldn't have come at the wrong time, needless to say, it gave me a weird vibe. Nothing seemed out of place as the waiter deliver my lunch. I said a quick prayer over the food once it was brought out before I dug in. The salad was the first thing to disappear followed by the grilled cheese and soup.

That is when I noticed a man walk in my direction; it wasn't until he got closer his facial features became familiar. Nervous and unclear of his motives, I did my best to remain confident and cool. There he stood tall and fine as wine with newfound facial hair. Dressed to impress, Joseph loved fashion so much he should have been a designer or something.

"Hello, Connie Wallace! I have dreamed of this moment for a long time," He flashed a smile as his cologne tickled my nose.

"Do you mind if I join you?"

"Have a seat," I motioned but wanted to tell him to go away but it would've been rude not to mention the butterflies in my stomach. It was evident his feelings for me never changed from the way he stared me down. If I was a menu item, he definitely would have ordered me.

He took off his black trench coat and laid it across the chair, unbuttoned his suit jacket and took a seat. "Please excuse my bluntness but how the heck did you get my number? We haven't spoken or had contact in years."

"Baby nowadays a few bucks can get me any type of information I want to know. You are a popular woman First Lady Wallace. It's nice to see you made a name for yourself. Married to a pastor with kids must be a nice life huh?"

"Umm, I guess, but it's more to being a wife and mother. We worked hard to get to where we are in life. Charles is a good provider, father, and husband."

"That is good to hear. Sometimes I wonder what our life would have been like had we married. You ever think about that?"

"Honestly, yes, I do. However, the past is the past and life goes on. I'm sorry things didn't work out between us, but they say things happen for a reason. Whatever the case, we cannot meet like this again nor can you send me messages as if we are buddies."

"Ouch. That hurt Connie! I assumed our bond couldn't be broken no matter the distance or time. It is clear that you have moved on with life but there is something we should discuss. When you broke things off with me, there was one little thing you forgot to disclose. A mutual friend I ran into mentioned your name and asked about our daughter, Tia."

My jawline tightened as I knew exactly what the discussion was about--his daughter Tia. It became very clear that his motive was to either blackmail me or threaten to reveal himself to Tia. "Joseph, women do things for a reason and sometimes there is no room for explanations. Yes, what I did was wrong but there is nothing that can change that choice now."

It was only fair to hear him out, so I patiently sat a little longer and ordered green bean crispers appetizer to snack on.

"Can you imagine how stupid I felt because it was news to me? I didn't know anything about a daughter until now. Now that we are face-to-face the anger has settled, there were so many choice words I wanted to shout at you."

Joseph went on and told me about his life journey since high school and how my absence deterred him from certain opportunities. It amazed me that the love of my life turned out to be the opposite of what I thought he would be. Charles wasn't in my plan, but it turned out God knew exactly what he was doing when he united us together against my will and better judgment. Saved by the bell, his phone rung which prompted him to get up to leave.

"I have to go but please believe this ain't over. I've got more to get off my chest. I'll be in touch." He slid on his coat and made an exit without looking back not one time.

The second he pulled off I felt safe enough to leave as well.

CHAPTER 22

ia Wallace

  In the passenger seat, I sat and thought about what transpired at the dinner table while Lance drove to his house. It was not my plan for him to witness what happened but then again, I knew better to invite him to dinner. Guess I was too naïve to believe my mom would behave herself on a holiday. Even worse, my dad was called out about going to the Landing Strip Lounge. Lance probably thought we were the family from hell even though he never said anything bad.

  Silently, I leaned my head back against the headrest with my eyes closed until the car slowly came to a stop. Lance parked, turned the engine off and exited the vehicle. He appeared on my side and pulled the door open as he took my hand to assist me. All I could do was smile. When we were together I was in my happy place, he made me forget about the bad days. It amazed me at how patient and accepting he was of me not to mention the baggage.

  "Tia look at me. Listen, no family is perfect so stop worrying about what happened. Parents aren't perfect and yes, they do and say crazy stuff sometimes."

  "I know but you just don't understand that this happens more than it should. It's wild that she will not acknowledge all the good I do. It's frustrating not to mention it hurts."

"You should go take a nice hot shower and then let me massage and lotion you down. We gotta get all that stress out of your body, only positive energy. Go on now get naked woman."

"You right, I'll be back."

When I exited the bathroom to join him in the living room, he was seated on a comfortable bean bag chair. The closer I got to him; I noticed he was rolling up two joints in rolling papers. It was apparent he knew just how much the dinner upset me.

"Wow, all this time I never knew you smoked weed."

"There is a lot you don't know about me, dear, but I'm willing to share if our relationship progresses. I want you to know everything about me including the fact my parents aren't perfect either. My mom knows about you, but she doesn't know you are African American."

My face frowned the minute his words hit my ears, but I didn't react or pop off because he had just witnessed my family drama. "Is there a reason she doesn't know or is it one of those complicated situations?"

"Yes, my dad is cool with it, but of course my mother believes that dating a woman who is not white is wrong. Scared of having a woman fall for my money instead of true love, she monitored the women I dated. Please know that you are who I want to be with no matter her feelings. When the time is right I want you two to meet but that is only if you want to."

"I can't even get along with my own mother; how can I do the same with someone who has an issue with my skin color?"

"I know, but who knows you can be the very person to break her."

"Miracles do happen huh? All I can do is try."

* * *

IN ALL HONESTY, I just knew he would find an excuse to not see me anymore but the more time I spent with him the more we had in common. It had been a month and I hadn't spoken to my parents in any form of communication. I felt like they both needed to get their life together before we could repair the damage. A work in progress myself, Lance had been a great supporter as the family squabble remained a chip on my shoulder. My relationship with my sisters never changed as we talked, FaceTime, and met for dinner a few times.

Thanksgiving made me realize that change was needed on my part. The first step in the transformation of my lifestyle was a little hard to adjust to. Money was not a problem. It was the idea of settling down and doing one thing. Teaching was a satisfying job that fit my professional persona, nothing shameful and I made a difference.

Lance encouraged me to take up a hobby; anything that didn't involve dance of course. The issue remained, what did I want to do with my life? For the first time in a long time I was lost, my purpose in life was unclear. At a point in my life, it was time to get serious in every aspect of life. To help me I started a journal for about a week and decided to turn my journal entries into a platform for those who felt the same way. When I followed up with Lance about it he decided to help me set up an Instabook account to target a specific audience. A few days later my side project entailed writing from the heart on different topics that folks could relate to.

CHAPTER 23

abrielle Wallace
Since I came out during Thanksgiving dinner, life had been great for me. The weight was off my shoulders. It had been two months, yet my mom still seemed a little hesitant to accept it. I had no doubt her love for me never changed. It was the idea that her perfect child wasn't just that, perfect. With both of my sisters out of the house, things were pretty quiet most of the time. It was odd for a few weeks being in our big house with only three people. Especially during mealtime.

I was out of school on winter break and it was really boring around the house with no one to chat with about random stuff. In the window seat adjacent to my bed I sat with my phone in hand. With my thumb I unlocked it and hit the FaceTime button to call Tia, bothering her seemed like fun. She answered with a bunch of smoke clouds surrounding her, all I could do was shake my head.

"Hey, sis! You caught me during recreational time," she laughed.

"I'm so bored in this house sis, come save me. Two more years and I'm out of here. It's so quiet in this big house

My parents did their best to support and accept me with their openness to attend certain events they otherwise wouldn't have frequented. The other night we all attended a play at the Milwaukee Amphitheater called It Gets Better by the Gay Men's Chorus of Los Angeles. The purpose of the plan was to bring awareness and strike a conversation about the issues individuals like myself dealt with. An eye-opener to those who were quick to judge instead of love, I prayed this educational moment sunk into the brains of my parents.

From the beginning scene, all the way through the message and songs incorporated made me laugh and cry. One young man confessed that he contemplated suicide on many occasions, however, therapy and his parents' acceptance helped him through. The stories shared of feeling lonely and abandoned broke my heart because no one should suffer in that manner. While the performance progressed, I told myself I had to be born for a reason, there was a purpose for me and hearing seven people's story helped.

During the ride home I questioned why God make me this way? Why did people have a hard time accepting me or any LGBT person? Therapy was always the first solution parents threw out in order to keep the family's image intact. It was hard to realize they couldn't force a person to be a certain way despite reputation or religion. Parents and religion made a difference in the future relationship between the child. I was thankful to have parents who didn't disown me because of my sexual orientation.

"Gabby sweetheart, thank you for insisting we attend that play. I learned so much tonight that never crossed my mind. Please forgive me."

"Dad it's okay. I'm just grateful you learned something and realized this lifestyle isn't a choice, it's who I am."

"Honey I agree with your father, forgive me for being so hard on you. Something's isn't meant to be understood. I love you no matter what."

"Thanks, Mom. Admitting what I was to myself was totally different than admitting it out loud to you all. I listened to the song by Indie Arie, Strength Courage and Wisdom, then decided to spill the beans. The weight of carrying that secret was so draining and depressing, but I never thought about suicide."

"Thank the Lord!" my mother shouted before my lips could close from making the statement.

"Live your life and don't live to please other people, Honey. Remember that we love you unconditionally."

No one fully understood that it's not as simple as labeling ourselves as male, female or transgender. Some days were better than others, but it took time. There were so many people who hid their true identity for the sake of others' feelings. As a person who did the same thing my goal in life was to start a non-profit organization to raise awareness and support the millions of people who live a lie every day. One thing was sure; I wanted others to be loved as I was, despite race or background. The stigma of suicide and LGBT studies were shocking, so much so, I had begun research. Empathy and respect were the two skills I wished all people possessed

One-on-one time with my parents gave me all the faith in the world to know others could change their perspectives. My parents didn't believe in shoving the bible in my face, instead we held our own bible study at the dining room table. I would highlight a few scriptures and give them my understanding of the message. Then I tried to make my parents see that as a lesbian I too was a child of God. Time alone with them actually taught me more about the two people who brought me into this world.

CHAPTER 24

L *auren Wallace*

Close to four months pregnant Azriah and I got an apartment together against our parents' will. Both legally grown we decided to make our own decisions since it was our lives. I'm not going to lie; life for us was far from easy at first because the cash flow was slow to come in. Within a matter of time, Azriah got a job paying $20 per hour doing IT tech support and troubleshooting. That allowed him to keep an eye on me as the pregnancy advanced. In love with him, marriage was the next big step to make us official in God's eye.

My father took my moving out the hardest because he felt like he let me down for whatever reason. However, I wanted my independence as a young woman. A child was never in my plan, but God saw otherwise, and it was a blessing for me to experience it. Everything happens for a reason and I believed having a child was the Lord's way of making me grow up. Beig first to get pregnant before Tia was scary because I'd always imagined her to be a mom. I sat on the couch while my baby cooked me a meal I'd been craving for all day. Just the smell of garlic bread had me swallowing as if I could taste it.

"Baby you want American cheese or parmesan on your spaghetti? The garlic bread is almost ready too."

"Just hook it up! I'll eat it however you fix it just hurry up." My cravings for everything drove Azriah nuts. All I did was eat, sleep, and pee in that order. Being with child was something I never wanted to experience again. Sure, each person had a different answer after having their first child. As for me, the body change was beyond amazing yet scary at the same time. Each time I went out somehow a baby book ended up in my cart. The female body was amazing.

* * *

MORNING SICKNESS WOKE me up before five Sunday morning which was the story of my life. Up long enough to sip ginger ale, Azriah had already been up doing some work on his laptop. Feeling better within the hour I kept contemplating if attending church was a good thing or not. I didn't want to face the head turns and stares but something in me wanted to hear my father preach. Within a blink of an eye I changed my mind and watched Joyce Meyer instead with a bowl of Frosted Flakes without milk. The bed and couch had been my new favorite pieces of furniture.

The morning turned into afternoon and when I woke from my third nap I had a missed call from my mom and a text from Gabby. They both inquired about setting a spot at the table for Azriah and me. The change in weather made me lazy but not lazy enough to go eat dinner at my parents' house. Regardless of my mom's disappointment in my choice, I knew she had a few containers of craving foods set aside for me. Ever since I moved out it seems like the visits are more pleasant.

By five, Azriah made it home from work which gave us plenty of time to arrive before the stove was turned off. Not knowing the menu items, my baby and I were ready to clean plates. Not in a mood to get dressed, jogging suits were all I wore until the maternity phase. I prayed not to catch heartburn though, oh my goodness that was the devil and kept me half the night. The minute I put my key in the lock the feeling of home overcame me with a warm feeling.

"Hey! We're here," I yelled as I slipped off my coat and Ugg boots.

CHAPTER 25

astor Charles Wallace

In my home office, I prayed to the Lord for peace and understanding. My family needed to be repaired--mended back to one. With Lauren gone the house was not the same and poor Gabby, seemed down without her sisters around. The amount of change that happened within a year made me shameful as a husband and father. Although word never got out to the church folks about the inner drama, it was only a matter of time before Deacon Black used it to his advantage. That fool made an announcement a week ago that his son and daughter in law were expecting.

While I sat glancing at the congregation's semi-shocked expressions, I too was surprised by his news. Lauren got engaged without telling me not to mention that little twerp didn't ask my permission. Without reaction, my jaw tightened then I looked over at Connie who had steam blowing from her ears. Quickly she smiled the second Deacon Black turned our way clapping. That was my cue to take the pulpit one last time before dismissing service.

That following Sunday Lauren and Azriah came by for dinner and eventually spilled the beans of their future moves. In such a sincere manner he gave his apologies to both Connie and me for not asking their permission first. He even went so far to pledge his commitment to us as his in-laws, reading the five commandments he created. Never had I seen a young man like him and it warmed my heart to know he loved my daughter. Her glow was proof of her happiness, even Connie behaved without incident. Gabby was excited to be an auntie and I a grandfather to a healthy girl or boy. In mid-conversation the sound of the door closing caught our attention then boom, there stood Tia.

Thank you, Jesus was all I could think as I jumped from my seat overjoyed by her presence. With a tight hug it was as if my prayers had been answered, the family together in a joyous moment. In awe, she greeted everyone. When it became Connie's turn their long embrace was evidence that prayer works. There wasn't any name calling or yelling at each other, just pure love and laughs. The girls shared their exciting news over dessert. Lauren announced her plans to take a few credits at a time until she could transfer to a four-year college. Tia then revealed she quit dancing and only teaches full time. I assume dating that guy was a factor in her decision. Unable to contain her emotions Connie shouted, "Thank you, Lord, you are the highest." For the first time in years, the Wallace clan looked and sounded like a normal group of people.

While I sat at the head of the table overlooking my family I admired their growth. In awe, time escaped us until Azriah pointed out how late it had gotten. Connie and I saw the kids outside to their cars and watched on as they drove away. "They grow up so fast, don't they? Our baby is having a baby."

"I'm not ready for all of that, Charles." I embraced her with a snug hug to reassure her things would be okay.

"Remember when Tia was about to be born? I wasn't ready for that, but you guided me. We will do the same for Lauren. Come on let's go inside."

"You're right. You almost fainted several times when her head peeped out of my cootie."

"Ugh, that forever changed how I view birth but gave me a newfound respect for childbearing." We went back inside and cleaned the kitchen as the conversation carried over to the bedroom. Nights together in that manner were those I cherished the most. We showered and cuddled to end the night.

* * *

MY MORNING WORKOUT in the weight room gave me peace and alone time. I spent fifteen minutes doing upper body. "Satan, we're gonna tear your kingdom down," I sang along to the Greenleaf TV Series Soundtrack on Apple music. I let the music use my body as I rocked back and forth praising His holy name. Life couldn't have been better at home and church, it amazed me how much improvement happened since the worst Thanksgiving dinner ever. Sunday dinners took a complete turnaround as Tia, Lauren, and Azriah joined us every week. Lauren's pregnancy became more and more acceptable to the point everyone couldn't wait to spoil the child once born. Towards the end of my workout, I glanced at myself in the mirror, grateful for transformation. Angela was a distraction who took me off course. The two times we had sexual encounters I let the devil use and abuse me.

On my way back upstairs to the bedroom, Connie was already up and in the shower. My mind in the gutter, I quickly went to the bathroom and slid inside. Without hesitancy, she submitted to me. Afterwards, we dressed and made it downstairs for breakfast before departing to the church. Connie decided to drive this time giving me time to recite my notes.

During the call to worship, I felt like a new reformed man with all of my priorities intact. Connie had even talked me into considering the Regional Bishop position, but it wasn't a for sure thing. Besides as bishop, that meant overseeing multiple churches, a task something a person like me had never done before. During choir selection the sight of Angela prompted me to keep both eyes far away from her. Sundays were strictly worship and family day. She knew better to expose us to anyone. Black folks were super nosy in our church and a rumor about me would do damage beyond repair. Either way our affair was all but over anyway.

CHAPTER 26

ia Wallace

While Lance attended a four-day conference in New York I called my sisters for a weekend at my house. I figured we could use the bonding time plus it had been awhile since our last sleepover. Each of us was in a good place in life leaving the drama behind in the past. There wasn't anything more fun than sister time, laughs, food, and gossip. Too lazy to cook a meal I ordered three pizzas, wings, and cheese sticks which were delivered minutes after their arrival. By the time they made it back downstairs, I had the plates and napkins out along with water and lemonade.

"T, this food is right on time cause I'm starving. That kid of mine keeps me hungry all the time."

Gabby grabbed more chicken than pizza and placed her plate on the table and sat. Chicken was her favorite food besides the french fries she ate all the time. "So what's been going on with you, sista girl? How is school?"

"Almost over praise Jesus! I'm so ready to leave for college and be on my own.

"Y'all heffas left me in that big house by myself. No for real, all is well just ready for a new start."

"Yeah we know the feeling little one but just wait patiently. Once you out the house adulthood kicks in starting with you footing your own bills. But in your case, mom might spoil you more. Either way, enjoy it all and make sure to network. College is a different ball game but you're a Wallace, so it will be a breeze." I reassured her with a smile then stuffed pizza in my mouth.

"While you asking us all these questions, what is going on with you and Lance? I'm all in ya business because I need to know," Lauren joked then stuffed a chicken wing in her mouth with raised eyebrows.

"Umm, as the big sister asking questions is my duty, ma'am. If you must know, Lance and I are doing well. He is making great efforts to give me the world, but I found out his mother is racist. How am I supposed to deal with that? You are the first to hear this so don't tell Mama."

"What? That is crazy. I will never understand folks like that. All I suggest is keep your distance when possible and try to avoid cursing her out." Lauren always had the advice to give me and I was grateful for that. More talk and laughter amongst us led time to creep up. Close to midnight we were full and laid out in the living room with the TV on laughing and chatting. Sisterhood couldn't have gotten any better than it was, we three together felt like the old days.

Up by six the next morning, I rolled up a joint and placed it behind my ear as I quietly went to the kitchen. In the mood for Yogi Tea, I filled the kettle with water and sat it on the stove. Gabby joined me soon after looking for something to eat as she searched the fridge first followed by the cabinets. She found Quaker's Oatmeal and proceeded to fix her some. Once I pour up my cup I passed the kettle for her to use the leftover water. Together we enjoyed each other's company at the counter. Sometimes silence was the best dose of medicine for some folks as Gabby didn't have much to say. I removed myself and went to the sun porch for my morning toke session. Stoned, I sat and people-watched for a good thirty minutes before my sisters found me. We spent the next two days shopping, bowling, and lounging around like bums.

* * *

I WAS EXCITED to see Lance. The house was cleaned, and dinner had already been prepped. After two o'clock in the afternoon, the mail carrier had run with a bunch of bills and junk mail. As I sorted and tossed most of it in the recycling bin, a letter addressed to me caught my eye. I didn't recognize the sender's name or address, so my face frowned from confusion as I opened the envelope. The white piece of legal pad paper was folded with my name on the top. Not sure what to expect I took a seat at the round cherry wood table. When I opened the documents, the neat cursive handwriting made me even more curious, it read:

Hello Tia,

You don't know me so let's just say I'm an old friend of your mothers from back in the day before she met her husband Charles. We used to have a lot of fun together until she was ordered to stop seeing me. As you can imagine that didn't sit too well with me but there was nothing I could do at the time. But when Connie told me she was pregnant I couldn't help but wonder if the child was mine or not. To make matters worse, she up and got married and moved. For years I search high and low without no luck but then to my surprise I found her again this past Thanksgiving.

I'm someone who would like to meet you soon to explain myself. I know you are wondering how I got your address and why I sent this letter. Well, it's possible you are my daughter and the suspicion is driving me insane. I already confronted your mom and of course, she denied the possibility however the timeline adds up too well. Please forgive me for dropping a bombshell like this but I have the right to know the truth. The only way to clear this up is to do a DNA test, in the words of Madea, DNA doesn't lie. Think about it and give me a call at 414-437-6467.

Look forward to hearing from you but in the meantime, ask your mom a few questions about her past. If she avoids the questions or answers around your questions, it's obvious she's hiding something. Until next time!

Sincerely,

Friend of the family

I dropped the paper as tears welled up in my eyes, there were no words to describe how I felt. A stranger who claimed to be my real father was the last thing I ever expected. My relationship with both parents had just been mended with past discretions behind us. In shock, it was never a doubt that my dad was just that--the man who raised me from birth until now. I placed both hands on my forehead and closed my eyes momentarily then removed myself from the table. My day had been officially ruined along with the dinner. In a numb state, my legs guided me downstairs in the basement for a smoke break. That was definitely a time to inhale some herbs and put my thinking cap on.

Each time I toked, the words in the letter took me back to childhood, a time when I never paid any attention to my father's physical looks or genetics. My facial features didn't resemble his, but we shared a bond that is why I never questioned the notion. On the verge of baked, I didn't even hear Lance enter the home until he stood before me.

"Oh, my goodness! You just scared the fudge out of me," I jumped and placed my hand over my heart as it beat rapidly. He had the envelope and letter in his hand with an emotionless face. Lance never really expressed his emotions about anything unless he was absolutely pissed about something.

"Hey, baby I didn't mean to startle you. I told you about smoking without having the cameras on down here. Aye, what's this all about?" He approached me leaning in for a kiss then sat next to me.

"Read it if you want, I'm too high to care. I'm just glad to have you home."

"I already did and whatever happens with the situation I got your back, never forget that!"

"You are too good to me! Can you imagine, learning something like this now? My mom is a real piece of work for keeping this from me. Do you think my dad is aware of this?" So many questions lay at the tip of my tongue leaving me lost about who I really was as a person.

Slowly, I leaned over until I was practically laid in his lap. He ran his fingers through my hair sending the most amazing feeling throughout my body. We spent maybe ten minutes in that position until we went back upstairs. He told me about his trip while I washed my hands then hooked up fried chicken, potato salad with a little macaroni and cheese. In the cooking process, Lance set the table then disappeared to clean up and change clothes. By myself, the letter haunted me again distracting my attention for a second. Let's just say we almost had some crunchy ass potato salad; egg shells and all.

Lance made his way back to the kitchen just as I had begun to turn off the stove. I put the mixed pieces of golden fried chicken in a large bowl and removed the mac to keep the creaminess. The only thing missing was white bread and Louisiana Red Hot sauce. We sat and enjoyed the quick yet tasty meal. It amazed me how much of a homebody I became with him around. Life was always full of surprises.

* * *

TWO WEEKS LATER, I decided to invite my mom to Denny's as a way to interrogate her based on the letter. We didn't even acknowledge Thanksgiving because we were way past that incident. Lance suggested instead of confronting her head on, be easy and watch her body language. He assured that her behavior to certain questions would help me figure out truth from a lie. There were some questions that needed answering and she was the only one who could provide them. Mr. anonymous came out of the blue with accusations causing unnecessary drama.

When I pulled in, her car stood out to me because she had different license plates. Confused, I wondered why she changed them after all these years. With a shake of the head, I got out and walked inside to join her. "Morning Mom, or should I say Ms. New Me, according to the plates!"

"Let's say midlife crisis and the need to change. How have you been doing?"

"Wonderful. Teaching more and enjoying life with Lance. We've been discussing our future. Speaking of the future, I want to make sure we can be honest with each other." A young lady appeared to take our orders then left to get the beverages before leaving us alone again.

"Tia, we don't have the best connection, but honesty has never been an issue. What's on your mind?"

Those words made me forget the entire game I was going to play but I needed answers. I opened my purse and pulled out the letter holding it in my hand looking her straight in the eyes. "Actually, this has been on my mind for a few weeks now. It's a letter from a man claiming to be my father. Care to chime in on that?" A pro at deception, I watched everything from her throat, eyebrows, to the movement of her body.

"Say what now? Let me see that," she said then snatched it from my hand to quickly read it.

While her head was down deep into the words on the paper, I noticed her hold back emotions. That was a telltale sign that those words did hold some truth after all. When her head raised it was written all over her face, she didn't have to say anything. Saved by the waitress, she placed our plates in front of us leaving us to enjoy the meal in peace. I spread the butter across the triple stack of pancakes and then lightly poured syrup on them in a zigzag motion.

"So, Mom you got quiet. Did something stir up memories or something? Not trying to start trouble, but he seems sure about what he's talking about. Tell me something, anything, otherwise, I'm going to call him to hear his side."

"Remember our lunch date at Bayshore Mall, we had a great time and you said something about doing things that I would never understand. Is this what you mean by that?"

"I said that?" she managed to mumble through a mouthful of her breakfast. Answering a question with a question was another sign she was hiding something. I came to my own conclusion that the mystery man was my biological father.

"It's all good, your body language basically answered my question anyway. Don't matter to me because the man who raised me is my father. It's just shocking that the woman who always preaches to me about stuff has been hiding the biggest secret."

"Tia that was a different time in my life and there are things you don't know, so you won't understand. Yes, I should have told you but at the time it didn't seem worth mentioning. Then we became heavily immersed in the church leaving me the option but to conceal that detail without revealing. Can you imagine the scandal and backlash this family would've endured?"

"How would that have happened by telling me, your daughter the only person who needed to know? Mom, please don't try to explain, I'm over it I just wanted to ask you in person. Oh, one more thing. Does dad know about all of this?"

"Not to my knowledge," I quickly lied. "Like I said this has been a secret for over twenty-something years."

I looked at my Apple watch as if I really had to be somewhere else. "Well, I gotta go grade papers and prep lunch and dinner. I'll take this back, thanks." I took the letter and stuffed it back in my purse. Her eyes followed my hand movement until the paper disappeared. In an odd headspace, I didn't want to be disrespectful given the choice of words ready to flow from my mouth were far from appropriate.

"Have a blessed day Mother." I left out the door not looking back once because I didn't want her to see the tear fall from my face.

Inside the car, I sat for ten minutes replaying breakfast with my mom and how she made excuses. I still didn't have a name or any other background information about the man, so I decided to text him. What was the worst that could happen? I pulled out the paper with his number and entered them into the keypad of my phone.

Me: Hi this is Tia and I got your letter. Even though I don't trust you I'm curious to hear your side of the story. I met with my mom and showed her what you wrote, and it definitely bothered her. Can we meet at a public place downtown somewhere? Let me know.

Finally, in the house, the first thing I did was plop on the sofa and grabbed the remote. All I wanted was a few minutes to unwind before getting those papers knocked out. When the television popped on the channel was on Animal Planet, a favorite of mine. There were so many educational shows on that station, in particular Pitbulls and Parolees. It was basically about giving abused and abandoned dogs a second chance in hopes of adoption. It was the same thing for the parolees who worked with the dog. It was a way to learn responsibility and redeem themselves. Some of the men get second chances and made a positive change.

Ding! the message alert sounded prompting me to grab my phone. It was a response from the man. Nervous to read the entire message my thumb clicked to open the envelope.

414-437-6467: I'm glad to get a message from you, Tia. Your mother is a great deceptive woman who said the right things at the right time. I truly loved her but a lie this big was unforgivable. Send me a date, time, and location and we can talk about whatever floats your boat.

Me: I want to meet you tomorrow at Elsa's On the Park around 4 pm. I will be sitting by the window dressed in a white and black coat. However, you need to reveal a name, or something given you're a stranger. I pressed the sent button and waited to see if he would respond right back. Sure enough, the grey bubble and three dots appeared as he typed a message back.

414-437-6467: Hello Tia! Look forward to meeting you in person. For now, you can call me Joe. We can discuss more in person. Bring an appetite because we have a lot to discuss. See you tomorrow at 4 pm sharp.

* * *

BUTTERFLIES FILLED my stomach when I exited the car headed into Elsa's. When I entered it appeared I beat him which made me feel semi better. Not packed yet, it was no problem to find a spot for us in an open space. A few minutes early I decided to order a shot to calm my nerves. I sat with my iPhone in hand as my eye watched the door every time someone entered. Occupied on Facebook I didn't notice Joe slip in until the motion of a person stood directly in front of me.

My mouth dropped from surprise as the man who stood before me was my identical twin. There was no way in hell my mother could dispute it either. In shock, no words came out my mouth. Scary was an understatement given it was like looking in a mirror at a stranger.

"Wow, this is unreal right now! Tia Wallace in the flesh, damn you are my daughter without a doubt. Is it too much to ask for a hug?"

Cautiously I embraced him but quickly released myself from his grip to sit back in my seat. The features we shared from the nose to the slight slant in our eyes let me know we were about to talk for hours about everything under the sun. For the first time in a long time, I was left without a snappy comment or anything witty. Instead, I remained civil and ordered eight chicken wings with onion rings and another drink.

"Oh, baby girl you're gonna need more than eight wings and one drink cause we're gonna be a while. I have some stories about yo mama." I flashed a smile then added to the order. Sitting with a stranger should've felt more dangerous or uncomfortable yet it was the opposite. He shared a few things I wasn't aware of about my grandmother in the process. All in all, I left with a new perspective and more questions.

CHAPTER 27

onnie Wallace

     Feeling lousy and unable to leave the bed, Charles checked on me one last time before he left for church. He made sure there were honey cough drops, Kleenex, and orange juice on the nightstand. Wrapped in a blanket all I cared about was sleep. There was nothing on my agenda to complete therefore the bed was my best friend all day. Nodding in and out most of the morning was great, however, I became a popular person in the afternoon. First Juanita called to check in, then Lauren called about a baby question followed up by Charles. Not one for having my sleep broken, I dragged myself out the bed looking and feeling like hell. First, I thought a shower would help but it didn't, so I forced some chicken noodle soup.

    It wasn't often I had a chance to bum around the empty house, so I set up on the couch in front of the 50-inch television set. I watched everything from Steve Wilkos Show to Dr. Phil and then I discovered Vh1. Oh, my lord it was appalling to see so many young women degrade themselves on camera. Even though I shouldn't have, I watched an entire season of Love & Hip-hop Atlanta. It got so good that I forgot all about being sick and got lost in the ratchetness until my phone went off again. At first, I ignored it until the reminder beeping sound made me pay attention. What I saw on the screen made me throw my phone across the room out of anger yet the only person to blame was myself. The entire evening from that point forward put me in a bad mood and I was glad to be in an empty home. I grabbed a bottle and the wine opener and went to my room.

* * *

"CONNIE, what in the devil is wrong with you? You haven't been acting like yourself lately and it's becoming an issue. Did you forget you are the First Lady?" He removed the Stella Rosso Red wine bottle

"Charles please don't start with me. Life is rough so to cope I had a little wine.

"You really want to know what's bothering me, Charles? Huh! Here, this is why!" I shoved the phone in his face, so he could see the picture on the screen. It was a photo of Tia and Joe together smiling. The image was proof that the relationship Tia and I had repaired was over for good.

"Oh boy, they actually met up. Did you know about this?"

"Tia told me she didn't care about him or the situation for that matter. It led me to believe she wouldn't go through with it." Charles sat down in the soft gray chair at the foot of our bed with his back faced towards me. I knew his feelings were hurt regardless of him knowing the truth about Joe. He loved and raised Tia from day one making her his baby girl no matter the circumstances.

"Connie, did Tia find out that I was aware Joe was the father? Oh, my goodness, she is going to hate me for lying to her. This cannot be happening." He let his head drop into his hands making me feel worse than I already did. Both Charles and I knew it was possible for Tia to find out the entire truth, yet not from Joseph. Tia was super pissed at me and the last thing I needed was for Charles to hate me too. In an effort to comfort Charles, I moved close by and sat in the chair next to him. Silent at first, I just glanced at him a few times then gained the courage to speak.

"Charles please don't hate me for all of this. My actions years ago have torn this family further apart than together. You had just mended things and here I go fudging them up. Honey, I swear in my life I had no idea this would happen."

"How did he find Tia anyway? For him to just appear like a ghost is strange to me. Yes, he has the right to know about his child and if it was me I might 've done the same thing. After all, he didn't even know about Tia."

"Wow, so it sounds like you're taking his side now." I shot up from the chair not able to believe my ears. He stood too and continued facing me.

"In a way yes, I am because he was denied the chance that I was given. Please don't take my words out of context Connie but just think. Before you blame your mother, you could have still informed the man--gave him the choice. All I'm saying is that actions result in consequences. As a pastor, my track record is far from clean, look at the Angela situation. We overcame that, so I know we will get over this hump."

"You know to never mention her name in my presence, ever! I get it and the matter will work itself out. Beginning now I'm not going to worry about it because Tia is a grown woman. What can't be fixed by prayer is just the way life was supposed to unfold." Just then Charles went into his pocket and pulled out the ringing phone. The ringtone distinctively repeated *daughter calling*.

"Is that Tia?" I stared him down as he nodded his head up and down then jetted to the bathroom closing the door behind him. Offended, I sat anxiously wondering why he had to go to the bathroom to talk. All of sudden, my phone vibrated rapidly on the nightstand. By the time I had it in my hand the vibration stopped.

The missed call from an unknown number led me to believe it was Joseph calling to inform me of his meeting with Tia. Seconds later, it vibrated again so I answered. "Hello. Joseph, is this you? If it is, please stop calling me." I could hear the anger in my voice. Faced towards the patio I listened to what he had to say.

"Connie sweetheart that's no way to talk to the father of your child. Tia is such a beauty, who knew we looked like twins. Anyway, I just wanted to let you know Tia and I will be spending more time together catching up."

"That is good for you. Please don't text me anymore since there is nothing to be said between the two of us. You found your daughter and if she accepts you so be it."

"If I didn't know any better you sound bothered. You know all of this could've been avoided. Denying me the right to know his child is cold Connie, especially for the First Lady of a church. I wonder what the lovely people of Calvary would think about their pastor and first lady?"

His words sent a chill down my spine as I got a weakness feeling. I prayed he didn't reveal this to anyone from the church. "Listen, Joseph, I did what I had to do at the time, you know how my mother was. She didn't feel like you were marriage material, so I was forced to marry Charles. Once that happened life went in a different direction for me, there was no way anyone could find out Tia wasn't Charles daughter."

"Nevertheless, you still could have let Tia and I know when she was of legal age. You made the decision for both of us and that, I can never forgive you for. Oh, and don't worry I'm not dirty enough to reveal this to the congregation. Sooner than later you will do something else to expose yourself. When this call ends, you won't hear from me again. Have a good life Connie. Goodbye."

"Who were you talking to?" I turned around to find Charles standing there with a look I'd never seen before. He looked like he had just lost his best friend and wanted to ring my neck all in one expression.

"Honey, you won't believe it but that was Joseph. He called to gloat and then let me know he wouldn't bother us anymore." Charles stared at me with his red puffy eyes without a word then just let it all out. When I opened my mouth to continue speaking he put his hand up to silence me.

"Sit down and listen. Don't speak until I tell you to either. I cannot blame you for loving another man and for having his child. I was aware of the situation when we got married and it was okay with me because no matter what Tia will always be my daughter. Why couldn't you have just told her the truth? Huh?"

His stern voice made it clear he was pissed off. I watched him pace back and forth torn, made me realize how much I fudged up with him and Tia. That was one time I didn't have an answer. Seeing him hurt made me wonder what was said on the phone between him and Tia.

"Charles, what can I do besides say sorry?"

"Nothing. Nothing at all Connie. Tia asked me if I knew about the Joseph situation. I was faced with the decision to lie or tell the truth. Guess what? She hates me too. I told her the full truth. I pray she forgives me one day and realizes my position in the matter."

"Still in my seat silence filled the air as neither of us spoke to one another. Charles made his point very clear. I was an awful as a wife and mother. Without warning he turned and walked away leaving me alone in the bedroom. Frozen in place, I remained seated for hours until it turned dark and fell asleep.

* * *

"Mom, wake up! Wake up!" I heard a voice as my body shook in motion side to side. Groggy, my vision became clear enough to notice Gabby standing over me.

"Hey baby! I must have dozed off. What time is it?" In an attempt to sit up, a little pain in my neck caught me off guard.

"It's close to six in the evening. I just came home to find it dark in the house and when I saw your car it startled me. You okay?"

"I'm fine. Your father and I had a little disagreement, but everything will work itself out. Why do you go to the kitchen and get dinner started? I'll be down in a minute to assist."

"Alright. See you down there," Gabby said then gave me a kiss on the cheek before exiting.

I slowly stood to my feet and walked into the bathroom to empty my bladder. As I washed and dried my hands, the woman in the mirror wasn't the true reflection of me. The woman in the mirror made a lot of mistakes and this time I was unsure of how to make that change for the better. In the back of my head I wondered where Charles went and if he was with Angela. He made a promise that the mistake with her was over and done but my gut made me feel different. Nevertheless, it was a hurdle for another time but regardless a divorce was never an option for either of us.

* * *

I THOUGHT Charles needed a few days to cool down, but it had been almost two weeks since he actually spoke a full sentence to me. He had been spending more time at church and in the guest bedroom leaving me alone with nothing but lonely thoughts. Christmas was literally a few days away. There was so much to do at the church and at home. There was no room for me moping around feeling sorry for myself, life had to go on and Charles had to eventually forgive me. To get out of the house I decided to spend a few hours at the church prepping for the Christmas Program. I got out the Porsche truck with my navy suede Jimmy Choo handbag and proceeded inside the building.

ANGELA SAT at her desk typing on her computer wearing a pair of red glasses. She actually looked like a real assistant instead of flirting with my husband. Making my appearance known I stood in front of her with a smile. She raised her head and looked me smack in the face to acknowledge me. "Afternoon, Angela," I spoke on my way to my office. Not at the desk for ten minutes, something in my spirit kept nagging at me. Of course, I followed my first mind and called her into my office to confront her.

"Angela can you please step in my office for quick second? I have a question for you," I spoke over the intercom. Without hesitation she appeared.

"PLEASE DON'T INSULT my intelligence dear, I see the way you gawk at him even though he does his best to ignore it. Charles is a man and men let their eyes wonder from time to time. For all I know you two have probably even fooled around, either way I don't want to know about it."

"Mrs. Wallace, I don't know why you have a vendetta against me but it's not ladylike to be so jealous. Your husband is a very fine man who does not sleep around, I'm almost sure of it."

"Excuse me if I don't believe a word you speak, I'm a woman who has been around awhile, my gut doesn't lie. I know my husband and he is sleeping around with someone. Believe what's done in the dark will come to light. you better hope you telling the truth." I couldn't believe the words coming from my mouth, in the Lord's house no less.

"Like I stated before, I'm not the woman you're looking for. On a serious note, I'm disappointed in the way you came at me here in the church. For such a classy woman, you just behaved in such a tacky manner. Now if you'll excuse me, I have errands and a meeting to attend."

I watched her walk away back to her desk. She closed her laptop and gathered her jacket and purse before disappearing out of my sight. She was right, I was tacky for speaking to her the way I did. In that moment, Charles walked about and had just missed the confrontation by a few minutes.

"Charles can we please speak briefly?"

"Not now Connie, I have a meeting to get to, but we can discuss whatever you want in the next hour."

"Hum, same meeting I just saw Angela leave for?" My statement was full of sarcasm, but he didn't bother entertaining it.

"Yes, that meeting Connie, I am a pastor remember? I'll be back.

It didn't make sense to even respond to him, instead I went to my office to think. My original plan to work on the Christmas program had been deterred by the Angela situation. Instead I headed back home. Ready to confront Charles about his extra activities I sipped some wine to pass time.

The sound of the garage braced me for his entrance. In the kitchen at the island, I decided not to cook a darn thing. He could eat an air sandwich for all I cared. The minute he spoke I just went in on him. "Angela and I had a good chat earlier while you were at your meetings. She shared a few things with me that were fairly interesting."

"Oh really, I thought you didn't like her? What did you two talk about?" Instead of sitting still and look at me he moved around the kitchen in efforts to avoid me.

"I don't have anything against her other than some of the outfits she wears. Anyway, she said there is a guy she has the hots for but there is a dilemma. The guy is married."

"What? I mean she doesn't seem like the type of woman to get involved with a married man. Did she tell you anything else?"

"We are not best friends Charles, she only disclosed basic information." His curiosity raised my eyebrow because he acted as if he was mad Angela had an interest in a man. It was obvious he felt some type of way. I was far from dumb, their interactions were a clear sign to me. Either way he knew better to let his discretions ruin our place in the church.

"Well that is her business. If she wants to live life in that manner who are we to judge. We have our own situation to resolve."

"You are absolutely correct," I stated then got up from the chair to leave the room. I no longer wanted to look at his lying behind otherwise an argument would've brewed. To ease the tension, I went to a more secluded area of the house for a little reading before bed. I had to hit the ground running the next morning in order to complete the Christmas Program.

CHAPTER 28

*C*harles Wallace
  Connie had become a person I didn't know anymore but that could be said about me too. I almost had a heart attack when she brought up Angela and the conversation they had. It was no way possible to know if Connie knew the truth or not so there was only one thing left to do. Earlier that day on Christmas eve I met with Angela one last time to let her know we had to officially break things off.

"Charles your wife asked me questions, questions as if she knows something."

"That is why I'm here Angela. We need to end this affair now because my family is falling apart. My intention was not for this to happen more than once."

"I won't lie, my intentions and advances were planned but I must respect your wishes. A married man with a conscious only means you really care about Connie. I respect that."

We embraced each other, it was clear neither of us wanted to say goodbye to the intimate moments. For the sake of my soul and marriage I had to right my wrongs. In agreement we parted ways with dignity and no harsh bitter feelings. However, by the time I made it back home, Connie greeted me at the door. She threw a balled up piece of paper at me and walked away to the kitchen. I had just ended the affair and there was no evidence either. Imagine my shock when I bent down to pick up the paper and unbaled it. Frozen in that same spot, the content made my mouth drop and suddenly I felt my heart pounding through my throat.

DEAR MRS. WALLACE:

The day you confronted me about Charles, you were right all along. I stood in the church and lied to your face. It's not something I'm proud of either but I must come clean before leaving town. That is why I'm writing to let you know things have officially ended between us. He came by my place earlier to make sure I understood. He is determined to make things right with you. Find it in your heart to forgive us, not because I asked, but because you will be able to move on without hatred in your heart. Again, woman to woman, I'm sorry.

Sincerely,

Angela

Unsure if it was a good idea to go talk to Connie, I went down to the basement instead. Mixed with emotions, I reflected on the recent events and couldn't be mad at anyone but myself. In a way it was commendable for Angela to confess to my wife but it was also an eye opener. From that night, I made a vow to myself and God to do better, or step down as pastor. The people needed a true leader, one that walked the walk and talked the talk. Baby steps made all the difference between Connie and I. She suddenly remembered her sin was just as bad as mine.

* * *

I MOVED from the guestroom back to suite with Connie. Moving back was a white flag sign, all I wanted was peace in the home. I had a flashback to the sermon I gave while in Atlanta, the words echoed in the back of my mind prompting me to revisit Romans 12 and

Proverbs 4:23. Alone I read those scriptures aloud a few times and it finally dawned on me. I realized the only way for me to repent was to walk by faith instead of fear. My trust in God needed to be stronger, my faith needed to be stronger.

Going into the New Year people made all kinds of resolutions: to eat better, get more sleep, work harder and a host of other things. New year resolutions were a chance to start 2018 off with a clean slate. In my case, a main resolution for me was to mend my family. Tia hadn't spoken to me since she found out about her biological father. I prayed by the time Lauren had the baby, a fresh wave of happiness would come to the Wallace family. Time heals all wounds they say, so until then all I could do was take each day as it came.

Evening service started at ten, my goal was to have everyone out of church within an hour. Safety was a concern given the drunks and violence took affect once it got dark outside. A quarter to seven I left my office and joined the congregant's upstairs, the extra time I made sure the mic worked and water was behind the pulpit. Anything short of a miracle, Tia and Lance showed their faces.

"AMEN!" I shouted as a few heads turned in my direction. Pure happiness to see her made everything alright. Ten on the dot, I opened with a prayer first, then welcomed everyone to the Lord's house. Gabby took my cue and came up to the podium to read scripture from 1 Chronicles 16:11-12 followed by Ms. Jackson who requested to read Proverbs 3:5-6. Afterwards one of the newer members, YaYa, wanted to sing a solo. Her angelic voice was nothing short of amazing. Her solo song "A Little More Jesus" by Erica Campbell made folks clap, rock side to side and shout. No more than fifteen years old, she definitely had a future in singing. At the end of the song she even said a brief prayer for the children of the neighborhood.

"Church give Miss YaYa another round of praise for such a lovely song. We all need a little more Jesus in our lives. You know I'm right folks, I know I'm not the only one. Let me hear you say it church. I need a little more Jesus! Say it like you mean it." Once the congregation was alert I went straight into the word, the sermon about change seemed befitting for the occasion. Instead of a scripted message I let the Lord use me as he saw fit.

"How many of you have your new year resolutions goals set already? I mean realistic goals that you can actually accomplish?" Hands went up in the air as folks scanned around to observe the others as I continued on. "Now church I know 2017 was a hell of a year for us all from the mass shootings, protest, and loss of life. The amount of chaos in the world is a sign that we need to get ready. One way of getting ready is to understand that our God has something better in store for us. We are his children and we are in duress. As Christians we face a lot of discouraging times that make us want to give up. But no church, that's not what God's soldiers do, we pray and give our battles to the Lord. Are y'all with me?"

"Amen, Pastor."

"With this new year less than two hours away, we have a chance to get right with God as a family. It is now that we should let go of the grudges, bad attitudes, and anything else negative. Let us go into 2018 fresh and clear minded on what we need to do to live a Godly life. So, make your resolutions achievable, hold yourself accountable and every day you wake up, praise His name. When you eliminate the baggage, you lift weight from your shoulders. Most importantly you unblock the blessings meant for you. Now that you've heard my voice I want to ask any brave souls to share with us your goals for 2018. If you feel moved come right up to the front and share your testimony."

Five individuals stood from their seats and made their way to the front. one of those five was my daughter Tia. My heart began to pound rapidly unsure what she planned to share. In one motion my eyes connected with Connie's as she probably shared my thoughts. I handed the microphone to middle aged man then took a seat careful not to display the worry on my face. By the time it came to Tia's turn I anxiously sat at the edge of my seat. When Tia took hold of the microphone my silent prayer automatically started.

"Good evening everyone. As you know I'm the eldest daughter of Pastor Wallace. It has been quite a while since I've been in attendance for reasons you don't need to know. However, as I sat and listened to my dad's words it made me realize that my goal to becoming closer to God should start now. As the daughter of a pastor life is far from easy. Scared to fail or not live up to the Wallace name always held me back from living the life I'm supposed to live. So, I guess what? I'm revealing to you all is that my goal is to get back into church regularly. I'm ready to stop playing and live a Godly life. So, I guess I'm asking for support and encouragement. Thank you."

Unable to fight the tears rolling down my face I quickly went up to Tia and embraced her. The words she spoke were sincere and it brought me so much joy to see her forgive me. "Honey I'm so sorry, please forgive me. I love you with every fiber in my bones," I whispered as Connie joined us. Caught in the moment of a miracle, I was able to get the service back on track.

Home safe and sound I thanked the Lord again for his grace and mercy while I undressed and slipped into my solid navy blue pajama set. Still on a cloud I watched Connie tie her hair remembering old times. I tried to reflect on how to improve our marriage given my indiscretions, the only conclusion was to leave the past and start fresh.

"Connie can I share something with you?"

"Go ahead."

"I love you! Please accept my sincere apology for the way I behaved, and the things said out of anger. Tonight was a perfect example that God answers our prayers. Tia showing up tonight was a statement that all can be forgiven. I'm glad to start the new year gaining trust from the women I love."

"Charles we've all done things and said things to one another out of spite. If you are willing to make amends, so I am too."

"I love you Mrs. Wallace!"

"I love you too Charles."

THE END

CPSIA information can be obtained
at www.ICGtesting.com
Printed in the USA
LVHW051628120419
613989LV00021B/500